The kiss was terribly ill-advised, absolutely foolish and irritatingly perfect.

Like he'd known it would be. The feel of Perla's lips on his had dogged him all day. And now here she was, perfect and soft in his arms. Kissing him with a hunger that set his blood on fire.

"I can't stop thinking about your mouth," Gael said as she grazed his neck with her teeth. "You're driving me wild."

"It's definitely mutual," she answered with a sexy little growl as she hooked her legs around him.

He'd told himself that she deserved better. Someone who could love her like she needed. Someone who could protect her heart. Told himself again and again that person couldn't be him. That his feelings for her were just fleeting infatuation.

But his reaction to her, the frantic hunger he felt for her, told a very different story.

* * *

Just for the Holidays... by Adriana Herrera is part of the Sambrano Studios series.

Dear Reader,

Welcome back to the world of Sambrano Studios! Where high drama is not just business, it's life. This second story follows Perla Sambrano, the youngest daughter in the family, as she gets her second chance at finding love with the man who once broke her heart.

In *Just for the Holidays...*, Perla finds herself snowed in at the luxurious Hamptons beach house of Hollywood heartthrob Gael Montez. Perla and Gael have *history*, and it all comes to a head when they have to pretend to be dating again for the sake of his family. But there is no faking it when it comes to the feelings that both have been harboring for each other. But Perla is still heartsore from Gael's betrayal years ago, and to get her back, he's going to have to earn her trust.

Thank you for coming into the Sambrano Studios series and this big, bold and passionate Latinx family.

Adriana

ADRIANA HERRERA

———

JUST FOR THE HOLIDAYS...

HARLEQUIN®
DESIRE™

Recycling programs
for this product may
not exist in your area.

ISBN-13: 978-1-335-73524-9

Just for the Holidays...

Copyright © 2021 by Adriana Herrera

All rights reserved. No part of this book may be used or reproduced in any
manner whatsoever without written permission except in the case of brief
quotations embodied in critical articles and reviews.

This is a work of fiction. Names, characters, places and incidents
are either the product of the author's imagination or are used fictitiously.
Any resemblance to actual persons, living or dead, businesses,
companies, events or locales is entirely coincidental.

This edition published by arrangement with Harlequin Books S.A.

For questions and comments about the quality of this book,
please contact us at CustomerService@Harlequin.com.

Harlequin Enterprises ULC
22 Adelaide St. West, 40th Floor
Toronto, Ontario M5H 4E3, Canada
www.Harlequin.com

Printed in U.S.A.

Adriana was born and raised in the Caribbean, but for the last fifteen years has let her job (and her spouse) take her all over the world. She loves writing stories about people who look and sound like her people, getting unapologetic happy endings. Her Dreamers series has received starred reviews from *Publishers Weekly* and *Booklist* and has been featured by the *Today* show on NBC, *Entertainment Weekly*, *O Magazine*, NPR, *Library Journal*, the *New York Times* and the *Washington Post*. She's a trauma therapist in New York City, working with survivors of domestic and sexual violence.

Books by Adriana Herrera

Harlequin Desire

Sambrano Studios

One Week to Claim It All
Just for the Holidays...

Carina Press

The Dreamers series

American Dreamer
American Fairytale
American Love Story
American Sweethearts
American Christmas

Dating in Dallas

Here to Stay

Visit the Author Profile page at Harlequin.com, or adrianaherreraromance.com, for more titles.

You can also find Adriana Herrera on Facebook, along with other Harlequin Desire authors, at Facebook.com/harlequindesireauthors!

One

I'm bored of playing the same character," Gael Montez muttered as he flipped through the pages of the script Manolo, his manager—and uncle—had asked him to review. "Is there nothing else I can do than play the 'ambiguously ethnic guy' in superhero ensembles?"

"*Ambiguously ethnic guy* parts in billion-dollar franchises make for a very good living," his uncle responded in that lecturing tone that put Gael's teeth on edge. "Space Squadron money is nothing to lift your nose at, mijo," Manolo continued, offering more unsolicited advice. "And this role has you as the lead, plus you'd get a producer credit. You're just in a mood this time of the year." The older man lifted his champagne flute, signaling to the private jet's flight attendant. Gael glanced away, annoyed that his uncle was right on both counts. His current gig as part of the cast of one of the most popular movie franchises ever was a dream job for anyone, *and* he hated Christmas.

Well, he didn't hate it exactly; it just brought back memories he'd rather forget. And he'd have to put his most cheerful face on by the time they landed, because there was no way he was going to put a damper on his mother's favorite holiday. Not after the year she'd had.

"I'm not in a mood." That got him a scoff from his sister, Gabi.

"You're always in a funk in December, Señor Grinch."

Gael bared his teeth at his sister, who loved to comment about his less than festive disposition around the holidays and every other "attitude" of Gael's she found lacking. Gabi lived to bust his balls. "I'm just tired," he sighed, and he felt it. Bone tired and depleted in a way that was starting to worry him. It was like in the past year he'd become completely numb. He did his work, and he did it well—Gael had high standards for himself and he never gave anything less than one hundred percent to any of his performances. He just couldn't get excited about *anything* lately. Maybe he was burnt out. Since his breakout role in an acclaimed cable series five years ago, he'd been working constantly. Offers just started coming in, and they never stopped. And having been raised by a single mom, who at times struggled to put food on the table, didn't let Gael even consider turning work down. He couldn't even remember the last time he'd taken more than a few days off to just do nothing. Maybe he needed a break.

He had the next ten days, at least.

The production schedule for the most recent installment of the Space Squadron—in which Gael played the brown guy with superpowers—allowed for time off from the press tours for the cast and crew for the holidays. Which was why Gael, Gabi and his uncle were on their way from LA to his house in the Hamptons, where his mother and the rest of their family would be spending Christmas. He was looking forward to not having to be "on" for the cameras 24/7.

He wasn't an ungrateful ass. He knew how lucky he was to have made it as far as he had. You didn't have to be in Hollywood too long as a Latinx actor to notice there weren't many others around. Never mind being cast for one of the most profitable movie franchises in the industry. On paper, he was living the dream. His profile was growing with every one of the movies he was in, and what was more, he was able to provide for his entire family. Hell, it seemed he employed half of them.

But five years into what seemed like movie after movie where his culture had no bearing—where his roots were some muddled inconsequential footnote— he yearned to take on a project that would show a different side to him. He had a couple of co-stars from Squadron—Tanusha, a Malaysian actress who was

his love interest in the movies, and Kwaw, a Ghana-
ian actor who was his friend off- and on-screen—
who had warned Gael about that, to not let himself
get pigeonholed as the "hot ethnic guy" in all his
projects. Kwaw already had indie projects lined up
before filming for the next Squadron, and Tanusha
was directing a documentary about the effects of cli-
mate change in her country.

Meanwhile, Gael was reading scripts for more
movies that only required him to flex his muscles
and look pretty. He tossed the script on the table and
took a swig of his own glass of champagne. "I'm not
interested in this, Manolo."

"Did you even read what the starting offer is?
It's more than what you're making with the Space
Squadron movies and you would have *the leading
role and an executive producer credit*. That's a great
opportunity."

"I've never heard of this production company,
anyone in this writer's room or the director. Looks
like it's a bunch of frat bros trying to make a buck off
the popularity of the Marvel franchises." That came
from Gabi, who for the past three years had been
working as Gael's publicist. It was a bit of Latinx cli-
ché to have his family working for him, but his sister
was excellent at what she did, and had a keen eye for
what was a good use of his time and what wasn't.

"Gabi, I appreciate your opinion, but I've been
doing this a bit longer than you have. I've been with
your brother from the time that no one gave him an
audition."

Gael scowled at Manolo's harsh tone. He loved his uncle and he was grateful for the support he'd given him over the years. It was true that he'd helped him get to where he was. That he'd been there every step of the way. But sometimes Manolo acted like Gael's abilities and talents were incidental. Like it hadn't been Gael busting his ass working two jobs while going to drama school. Or it wasn't Gael who ran from audition to audition from the time he was eighteen until he finally caught a break that last year of college. And he didn't owe that break to Manolo; that had been because of...well, that wasn't anything Gael would be rehashing, not if he wanted to show up at his mother's in a better frame of mind. None of it mattered anymore. What did matter was Manolo's high-handedness.

Gael turned to his sister, ignoring the glares she and Manolo were directing at each other, and pointed to the stack of screenplays he was supposed to look over. "What project do you think I should do next?"

"Nothing in that pile," Gabi replied, clearly ready for the question. "Gael, you're in a good place in your career. Money- and work-wise. You *can* afford to take on a passion project, bro." That earned her a sneer from Manolo, which Gabi completely ignored.

She was in more casual attire today, her usual designer power suits replaced by Gucci sneakers and a tracksuit—*a Prada tracksuit*, but nonetheless, it was dressing down for her. They may have been twins, but Gabi took more after their mother. She was short and very curvy, while Gael was tall and brawny. He'd inherited his father's bronzed skin and green eyes, as well as his height. Gael was well over six feet tall and made sure he stayed in Hollywood Heartthrob shape. It was part of his job to look the part, after all. Like his mother said, if the acting gig hadn't worked out he could've been right at home in an NFL defensive line.

What Gabi lacked in stature she made up by being a total hard-ass, and his sister was rarely wrong when it came to the moves that would push his career in the right direction. Whether Manolo liked it or not, Gabi had an instinct for this stuff.

In the family they'd always joked that Gabi had been born clutching her planner and with her iPhone to her ear. His sister worked hard and kept her finger on the pulse of what was happening in the industry. Manolo was more focused on the money side, on what kept the family financially secure. They both loved their jobs, and frankly, their jobs depended on Gael's staying employed.

That meant that when it came down to it, he always made the choice that guaranteed him—and all of them—security. That particular approach had cost him dearly through the years, but he was a realist, and when you had people depending on you like he did, you didn't always get what you wanted. Gael thought he'd made peace with that, but in the past year he'd started losing his drive. Taking every lucrative offer that came along was killing his passion for the craft. He needed something to rekindle the fire he'd always felt for acting. In theory, he had everything any Latinx actor at this stage in their career could ask for, and still he felt…dissatisfied.

And yet…there had been a time not too long ago when nothing and no one felt more important than career success. A time where he'd made choices that might've seemed heartless to some in order to stay on the path he'd set for himself.

"Did you hear me, Gael?" His sister's voice snatched him back from his thoughts.

"Sorry, what did you say?"

She sucked her teeth at him for daring to ignore her, but soon was talking excitedly. "Word is Violeta Torrejos just signed on to direct a period series about Francisco Rios and his wife. It's about their time at Harvard." Gael perked up immediately at the mention of the Puerto Rican freedom fighter who was one of his heroes. "They're still looking for an actor to play the lead." Gabi smiled knowingly as he sat up in his chair. That last morsel of information jolting him out of the ennui he'd been steeped in a second ago.

"No eso, no. I already told them this part's not right for you and—" Manolo protested, but Gael held his hand up, annoyed that Manolo had passed on a project like that without running it by him first.

"Tio, esperate," he interrupted and turned to his twin. "Tell me."

Gabi grinned icily at their uncle, then bent her head to scroll on her phone, presumably looking for the information she had on the project. "It's called

The Liberator and His Love. The showrunner is Pedro Galvañes."

That was a good sign. Galvañes's name attached to a project usually meant there would be a lot of buzz for the show. "They've cast Jasmine Lin Rodriguez as Claudia Mieses," Gabi informed him, eyes still on her phone screen. Also a good sign, Gael thought, excitement already coursing through him. He knew Jasmine and she didn't sign on to just any project.

Gael leaned back, considering the information his sister had just given him. It was exciting to think about. A series about Francisco Rios, the leader of the Puerto Rican independence movement, was a dream project. The man had led an extraordinary life. He'd graduated from Harvard Law School in 1921—the first Puerto Rican to do so. While studying there he'd met Claudia Mieses, a Peruvian biochemist—and the first Latina to be accepted to Radcliffe College— who was remarkable in her own right. Gael had always thought their love story was a romance for the ages. And that Rios's life story deserved to be told. Being a part of bringing something like *this* to the big screen was more than a dream…it was the kind of opportunity that had drawn him to be an actor in the first place.

"I want it," he said with finality, feeling a buzz of excitement he hadn't felt in months. "Who do we talk to?" he asked. Hell, he'd probably be willing to do the part for free. But his sister frowned at his question, her expression almost reluctant. When he looked at

Manolo, Gael noticed the man looked smug. Clearly, the other shoe was about to drop.

"The studio producing the series is Sambrano," Gabi blurted out, as if trying to quiet their uncle before he could get the first word in. No wonder the older man was smiling. What felt like a ball of lead sank through Gael. The skin on his face felt hot. He shouldn't be surprised that the mention of the Sambrano name still had this effect on him after all these years, but it did.

"Tell him who's in charge of casting, Gabriela." His uncle sounded a little bit too pleased with himself for that nugget to be anything other than the person Gael suspected.

Gabi fidgeted, her eyes everywhere but on Gael. "Perla Sambrano's doing the casting." Unsurprisingly, he felt the blood at his temples at the mere mention of his ex-girlfriend. Perla Sambrano was someone he took pains not to dwell on. "She's working for the studios now," Gabi added, pulling him from his thoughts. "She's their new VP of global casting and talent acquisitions." His sister's tone was sharp, laced with recrimination. Perla Sambrano had been the reason for the one and only time his twin had stopped speaking to him.

"I don't know if this is the right project," he said, ruthlessly tamping down the pang of discomfort that flashed in his chest. He stared at his sister, expecting her to rehash old arguments. But she just stared at him, disappointment written all over her face. He knew enough not to take the bait. That conversation was over and done with. He would not apologize for making the choices that had them all sitting in a private jet heading to the ten-million-dollar mansion his money had bought.

"This is not going to work, Gabi," he told his sister, before turning away from her withering glare. He looked at his uncle and felt a surge of irritation at the pleased little smirk on his face. He was not some damn toy for Manolo and Gabi to compete over. "These aren't going to work, either," Gael quickly added, gesturing to his uncle's pile of scripts. "Let's keep looking." That made Manolo's smile flag, but he wasn't here to save anyone's feelings. This was his career, and family or not, they worked for him.

Gabi nodded tersely. She opened her mouth as if to say something, but then seemed to let it go. Gael focused on the book he'd been reading on his phone and tried very hard not to think about Perla or the project.

Dwelling on ancient history was not a habit he indulged in.

"You really don't mind doing this?" Perla's older sister asked. Esmeralda's warm smile always seemed to calm her even when she could only see it through the screen of her monitor.

"Of course I don't mind," Perla said, honestly. She couldn't exactly blame Esmeralda for looking a little doubtful. A year ago no one, Perla included, would've believed that she'd be ready for a conference call at 7:00 a.m. on a Saturday two days before Christmas, but here she was.

To be fair, a lot had happened in the past twelve months. First, her half sister, Esmeralda, had taken up the helm as president of Sambrano Studios, the television empire their father, Patricio Sambrano, had built. The same television empire everyone expected to be passed to Perla and her brother—Patricio's "legitimate" children. Instead, the Sambrano patriarch had surprised everyone by expressing his last wish was to see Esmeralda, the child he'd fathered out of wedlock, lead the billion-dollar studios into the future. In the aftermath, Perla had gained a relationship with Esmeralda after years of estrangement.

Unlike her mother and brother, Perla didn't begrudge her sister the position. She'd never wanted that kind of responsibility. In truth, until ten months ago, when Esmeralda had reached out to her, hoping to mend their relationship, Perla thought she would never set foot in the company's offices again. She'd even sold her shares to make sure she never had to sit in a board meeting for the rest of her life. But Esmeralda's warmth and passion for keeping their family legacy alive had lit a fire under Perla. And now here she was, the new VP of global casting and talent acquisitions for Sambrano Studios. As her sister said, "putting to good use all that fancy schooling" their father had paid for.

"Perlita?" Her sister's soothing voice pulled Perla out of her musings, and when she looked at the screen, she saw that Esmeralda's fiancé and the

CEO of Sambrano Studios, Rodrigo Almanzar, had joined her. They sat side by side, shoulders and arms pressed together. Completely comfortable with each other. They made quite the power couple, but their chemistry was not reserved just for the boardroom. Esmeralda and Rodrigo were the very definition of *soul mates*. You only had to see them together to know they were perfect for each other. Even when they had been at each other's throats competing for the top spot at Sambrano, they could not stay away from each other. And although Perla would never be jealous of what her sister had, she did feel a pang of longing for that kind of connection.

"I'm ready," Perla assured her sister.

"And after this, no more working," Esme chastised, making Perla smile. "We've all been working nonstop."

Perla would never admit it to anyone, but it felt good to finally have this, family who cared about her without making her feel like a child. Family that didn't make her feel expendable.

Her mother, Carmelina, had always been overbearing and the worst kind of helicopter mom. She constantly made Perla feel like she was useless. But Esmeralda treated her like an adult. Like a competent, trustworthy adult capable of taking on responsibilities. And more than that, Esmeralda made Perla feel like her presence mattered, like she valued her opinion.

"Let's get on with this meeting, then." Perla nodded, getting herself in order. They would be doing a virtual conference call with the producer and director of an upcoming series project.

The conversation with the show producers started well, and before she knew it, it was Perla's turn to ask some questions about casting. "Pedro, I know you have such deep connections with some of the best Latinx actors," Perla spoke truthfully. Pedro Galvañes was a legend, and was also infamously vain, which was confirmed when he smiled widely at her compliment.

"We know who we want," Galvañes confirmed. "Violeta has pretty much confirmed Jasmine Lin Rodriguez to play the part of Claudia Mieses." Perla, Esmeralda and Rodrigo all nodded enthusiastically at that. The Puerto Rican actress was a rising star, especially coming out of her huge success with the *Carmen in Charge* series.

"That's wonderful. She's perfect for that role," Perla said, grinning, not even trying to hold back her excitement.

"Yes, she is," Violeta chimed in. "And we need someone who can really hold his own with her. Francisco Rios was such a presence, larger than life. We need an actor who exudes that charisma and power, but who can also play the part of romantic heartthrob. This is a romance, after all." She winked, eliciting a smile from Perla and the other faces on the screen.

"Yes, we need a powerhouse to play Mr. Rios," Perla agreed. She'd been reading up on Francisco Rios since Esmeralda announced Sambrano would be making *The Liberator and His Love*. The man was a legend, and they needed an actor with a lot of depth to do him justice.

"Who did you have in mind?" Rodrigo asked, not one to beat around the bush.

"We want Gael Montez," Violeta announced, and Perla's heart skittered in her chest like a caged bird. As if the very mention of the man aggrieved the organ he had so badly battered.

"Montez," Esmeralda said, and Perla could hear her sister's effort to sound neutral. One night after one too many glasses of champagne, Perla had confessed the entire sordid story about her college boyfriend and her first—only, if she was honest—love.

A story she tried extremely hard to never think about, and now it seemed she would be tasked with securing him for a role.

"He's perfect for the part. Strapping like Rios was, and compelling on-screen," Pedro said, before Esme could finish what she was about to say. "But we have not been able to get so much as a call back from his people. The man's manager is a real piece of work. He flat-out refused to pass on the script to Montez."

Over the thumping of her heart and rushing of blood between her temples, Perla was able to process the mention of Manolo Montez, Gael's uncle and manager. She'd never liked Manolo and had always suspected he'd had a hand in how things had ended between her and Gael six years earlier. She wasn't at all surprised to hear he was still running interference. Manolo was never shy about the intensely specific vision he had for Gael's career. And the plan seemed to be very much about keeping Gael's status as the family's golden goose by encouraging him to take whatever role paid the most money.

He was ruthless, too. If Manolo thought this wasn't the right kind of project for Gael, he'd do whatever it took to keep it off his nephew's radar. And the truth was this was a passion project for everyone involved. They wouldn't tolerate egos in this production. The hope was that the expected accolades and critical acclaim would be an incentive for the bigger Hollywood names they were attempting to sign on—Manolo would never see it that way.

And Perla should be glad for Manolo's shitty ways because that meant she wouldn't have to deal with Gael. Except the more she thought about it, the more she agreed with Pedro and Violeta's assessment that he was the right actor for the part. What was more, she knew this was the kind of project Gael would've loved to be a part of. In college, when he'd been the darling of the drama school, this would've been a dream for Gael. Being Puerto Rican, he longed to play the kinds of roles that allowed him to represent his roots, even if he'd decidedly strayed from that as his career took off. And like the fool she had always been when it came to that man, the words were out of her mouth before she could stop them. "Gael's a friend. I bet I can talk him into taking the part. I'll give him a call."

Esmeralda and Rodrigo's stunned silence was somehow louder than the delighted cheers coming from Pedro and Violeta.

Once the call was done Perla's pulse still raced as she reckoned with what she'd done. She'd practically assured them she could secure Gael. She hadn't seen or talked to the man in six years. Since he'd come to her apartment on Christmas Eve and told her he'd finish the last semester of school online because he'd gotten a role in a new show. Then he'd dumped her with the excuse of needing to focus on his career. Even after all this time, she could barely recall the details of what he'd said. The pain of his betrayal still fogging her recollection of that horrible night. She sometimes wished the same fog would blur the two years before that. That she could forget how happy she'd been with him. But the memories of what she'd lost were still intact, and just as insidious as the pain of losing Gael had been.

"You don't have to do this, hermana." Esmeralda's uncertain tone shook Perla out of her thoughts. "I'll call Violeta and Pedro myself and tell them they need to go with someone else." Perla felt queasy and furious at herself for still letting the mere thought of him get to her like this.

God, she could not believe she'd put herself in this situation. But this was just like her, to try and please people, even if it came at the cost of her own peace of mind. Still, this was her job. She oversaw the casting of this project, a show she knew could be the talk of the awards season next year if they cast it well. She wanted them to have the best possible actors, not just for the sake of popularity, but because Francisco Rios deserved to have someone in that role who understood the man they were playing. Who got the size of the shoes they were attempting to fill.

Perla smiled at her sister through the tightness in her throat, trying to express as much gratitude as she could for Esmeralda's wanting to make this easier. "It's okay, Esme. I can do this. I shouldn't have said I could talk Gael into taking the role," she admitted. "But I can give him a call." *Or give someone in his camp a call, because I don't know if I can handle hearing his voice. Or maybe I'll just dial up my old college roommate, who I iced out without explanation after her twin brother broke up with me.*

"If you're sure," Esme said, the concern coming through in her voice.

"I am." Perla attempted to infuse her voice with confidence, trying to reassure her sister and herself. "Honestly, it's not a big deal. Gael and I are not super close anymore, but we're not enemies." Friends didn't exactly go six years without speaking a word to each other, but Perla hoped her sister didn't know her well enough to tell she was lying through her teeth.

"Okay," Esme relented, but Perla clearly saw the concern on her sister's face. "But if you change your mind, call me." She waved a hand then, her eyes widening as if remembering something important. "Or better yet, you can tell me in person when you're here."

Perla's mouth tugged up at that. Last year had been the worst Christmas of her life—well, the second worst. Her mother and brother had shunned her after she'd gone against them by selling her shares

to the studio. The decision had thwarted their plans
to destroy her father's legacy, and they'd stopped
speaking to her after that. She'd ended up spending the holidays completely alone—in a Swiss cha-
let in the Alps, but still, alone. But this year she
was going to Punta Cana with Rodrigo and Esmeralda. Esme's mother and aunties would be there, too.
Perla had been looking forward to it for months. The
idea of being around people who actually wanted
her there, with people who liked being around *each
other*, made her chest radiate with warmth.

"By the time you wake up tomorrow, I'll be there.
I'm taking the jet out of Westchester. We leave at
11:00 p.m." She couldn't wait to be on the beach,
even though she'd miss the snow. She was a New
York girl, after all, and loved seeing a white Christmas morning. But this year the blanket of white
would have to come from the sandy beaches of the
Dominican Republic.

She said her goodbyes and sat there for another
minute, considering her options. She didn't know
what prospect would be worse, to call and have
Manolo send some lackey to rebuff her, or actually get a response from Gael. Just the possibility of
hearing his voice made her nauseated. She breathed
through the jittery energy that was threatening to
overwhelm her. There were no two ways about it—
and the more she delayed it, the worse she would look
when she had to break it to the production team that
she had not in fact been able to secure Gael Montez
for the project. She grabbed her phone and stared at

it for a long moment, considering what to say on the off chance she got ahold of Gael himself. Maybe it wouldn't be that bad? It was business, after all. Gael could not begrudge her trying to woo him to the project. It *was* her job. Yeah…it would be fine. She'd call, put forth the offer and hope they accepted.

Maybe if she kept telling herself that, she'd start believing the lie.

She tapped on her phone and the screen came to life with an image of Perla and Esmeralda with their arms around each other at the studio's holiday party just a week earlier. She had to do this. For her sister, and for herself. This was her job now. And dammit, she would do it. Gael would understand that better than anyone. How could *he* judge *her* for putting her job ahead of personal feelings after the way he'd treated her? Still, she couldn't help but send a prayer up asking for a Christmas miracle.

Just as she was about to search in her contacts for Gael's old number, the screen of her phone lit up with a phone number she never thought she would see again.

Two

"Gabi?" Perla asked, scarcely able to believe Gael's sister was calling her. Had she summoned her with all her fretting?

"Hey, Perla. Do you have a minute?" Gabi sounded more than a little apprehensive, and knowing that her old friend wasn't unaffected by reaching out after so much time eased Perla's nerves. The two of them had only spoken a few times since she and Gael split. The last time it had been when Perla found out Gael's mother was sick. Perla had loved Gael, but she'd adored his mother, too. Veronica was always good to Perla and when she'd heard the older woman had fallen ill, she'd called Gabi to ask if she could come see Veronica at the hospital. Gabi had been grateful for her concern and told Perla she could come whenever she liked, but other than that, she'd kept her distance. So yeah, this call was a surprise.

"Hey, how's your mom doing?"

"She's good. Much better, thanks for asking."

Perla could hear the smile in Gabi's voice. Both she and Gael were devoted to their mother. If there was a pang of longing tugging at her heart for the warmth and joy she'd experienced with the Montez family, Perla would ignore it. There was nothing for her there. Gael had made that very clear six years ago.

"How can I help you, Gabi?" She tried to sound nonchalant, but even she could hear she failed.

"I've been told you're in charge of casting for the Francisco Rios series." Gabi was nothing if not direct.

"I am," Perla answered, stretching out the words.

"Between you and me, Gael may be interested in the role." Perla's pulse kicked up like she'd been given a shot of adrenaline, and she could not for the life of her tell if it was because she was happy or terrified about what this could potentially mean. She didn't have time to dwell on it; Gabi's urgent tone brought her back to the conversation. "The issue's Manolo. He's hell-bent on passing up on it. Saying it's not going to be good for his image," she scoffed. "Whatever the hell that means. And like always, my brother listened to him."

Perla knew that it was a lot more than just Gael's listening to Manolo, his uncle. She knew Manolo had stepped in to care for their family when Gael's dad abandoned them, leaving his wife with ten-year-old twins to support on her own. Veronica, who had been a stay-at-home mom until then, had been forced to go to work. In a gesture of solidarity, her brother-in-law Manolo had packed up from Puerto Rico and helped raise the twins. Gael felt like he owed his uncle, and that was not something he took lightly.

But Gabi had also confirmed what she'd suspected: Gael wanted this role. And unless he was a completely different man than he'd been six years ago, she knew he would likely take it.

Gael listened to Manolo because as long as his uncle took care of the "business side" he could focus on the only thing he really cared about—his craft. Success was never really about the money for him; it was about mastering what he did, about reaching the very top of his field. The possibility of being a contender for a best actor nomination with a role playing a Puerto Rican legend would be too tempting for Gael, even if it went against his uncle's advice. More than anything, Gael wanted a legacy, and he had to know that superhero movies could only take him so far when it came to claiming his star on the Walk of Fame.

"What do we do to convince him?" Perla heard herself ask.

"We can figure this out!" Gabi responded, clearly excited. Her old college roommate had always been a little too willing to get up to mischief to get her way. "I think it won't take much, to be honest. He's intrigued by the part. Rios is one of his idols." Perla remembered that, like she remembered every detail about Gael Montez like they were burned into her brain. "Timing is the key here," Gabi said, bringing Perla's focus back to the task at hand. "He's got the next week off before he goes on the Asian press tour for Space Squadron. We're at the new house in Sagaponack. We got in last night with Tio Manolo, but he took off for the city first thing this morning and won't be back until Nochebuena."

Perla hummed in acknowledgment, her matte, blood-red gel tips tapping on the desk as she thought. She'd seen a spread in some magazine about the enormous ten-million-dollar Hamptons mansion Gael had bought for his mother. Not surprising they'd all be there for the holidays.

"What if you call him?" Gabi suggested cautiously. "I know it's a big ask, but he always trusted your advice when it came to his career." Perla could practically taste the bitterness that statement brought up. Gael *had* listened to her, until he didn't. And despite what she'd told herself a minute ago, she didn't think she could handle being rebuffed by some assistant. No, Gael owed her this, and if he was going to tell her no, he'd have to do it to her face.

"Why don't I bring him the script," she heard herself say, feeling a little floaty from the barrage of feelings the prospect of seeing Gael brought on. "I can tell him in more detail what we're envisioning for the show. We could even do a reading."

"Okay, if you're sure." Gabi sounded unsure.

"It will be harder for him to turn me down in person," Perla said, now sounding a bit more sure of herself. More committed to the plan.

"I like it," Gabi finally answered. "Having you here

will force him to consider the role seriously." Perla's pulse quickened as blood rushed through her veins. Seeing Gael was not a good idea. But she knew this was the right call. Once he read it, he would want it.

As if she could sense where Perla's thoughts were heading, Gabi piped up again. "Didn't Caballero-Mendez write the script?" Gabi asked, prompting a quick yes from Perla.

"Gael's been wanting to work on something by him for years." The Puerto Rican playwright had risen to supernova levels of fame after his musical based on the life of one of the US founding fathers had become the Broadway hit of the decade. Everyone wanted to work with him, but he only took on very selected projects.

"He *offered* to write the script for us," Perla clarified for Gabi, who crowed in response.

"Excelente. Wait to tell him that until he's got it in his hands," Gael's sister suggested with glee. "You're coming with an offer he can't refuse."

Perla had to breathe through the thumping in her chest as she prepared to speak. "Would lunchtime today be too soon?" Perla was already mentally listing what she needed to do before she got on the road. "I'm planning to fly out to Punta Cana late tonight, from Westchester. I can drive out to you before that and be back on the road with plenty of time to catch my flight at 11:00 p.m."

"Yes! I can make that work," Gabi was yelling into the phone. "You know he's a workaholic and already bored to tears with nothing to do. Send the script over now, and I'll print it out and give it to him. He has all morning to read it." She made another celebratory sound on the phone and Perla wished she could get some contact giddiness; alas, all she felt was nausea. "I have a good feeling about this, and Mami will be so thrilled to see you. We've all missed you." Gabi said that part in a more subdued—but no less genuine—tone. And maybe this would be a way to prove to herself she was past this. That the heartbreak from years ago was ancient history.

"I look forward to seeing her, too," Perla said sincerely, and after hammering out a couple more details they disconnected. Perla tried to push down the blizzard of emotions that seemed to hit her all at once. She was nervous. No. She was terrified of seeing Gael again. Not just because of how things had ended, but because she had no idea how she would react to having him in front of her. She wondered if it would still feel like the sun, the moon and the stars were encompassed in his green eyes. If it would still seem like he was the only person in the world who could make her fill up with light.

She reminded herself that she wasn't that lost girl, who in Gael had finally found someone who could see her. That she had people in her life now, and more important, she'd been working hard on loving herself. And she did; she'd felt more confident in this past year than she could remember. And despite all that being true, the longing she felt for what Gael had been to her was a yawning, undeniable void.

Seeing him was a risk; there was no use in denying it.

This was dangerous, treacherous territory she was threading into. But she *would* do this. If the old Perla would've cowered at the possibility of seeing the man who had broken her heart, this one would toss all that useless sentimentality aside and do her job.

Gael was going to kill his sister. He was at least going to have decidedly strong words with her. The fresca had barreled into his bedroom at barely 9:00 a.m. in the morning with a ream of papers and announced that no one other than Perla Sambrano was coming to talk to him about taking the lead role in the Rios series. Only the most brazen and fearless of people would dare talk to Gael before he'd had his coffee, especially with news he would not be happy about. But Gabi had always lacked a healthy sense of self-preservation. It was the only reasonable explanation as to why, without consulting anyone, his sister contacted his ex-girlfriend and invited her to his house.

And now here he was, standing in his driveway, waiting for the woman whose heart he'd trampled. Gael made no apologies for his choices. He was ruthless in his dedication and ambition—mercenary, his mother would say—and he had no regrets. The only way that a kid from Bridgeport, Connecticut, had been able to achieve what he had in such a short time was because he never let his emotions get the best of him. Even if that meant breaking the heart of someone he'd loved.

Perla had been his sister's roommate freshman year at Yale. And then she'd become much more than that. In the summer between sophomore and junior year, Perla and Gael had started dating. She'd been the first girl he'd fallen head over heels for. They'd had two almost perfect years. She'd been more than his girl-friend; she was his best friend, his confidante. The person he came to for everything. And when his career started taking off and he'd been overwhelmed and intimidated by the entertainment business, she helped him navigate the new world he'd been thrust into.

It was her playground, after all. Perla had grown up in the lap of luxury. The "pobre niña rica" as his friends sometimes called her. She *was* rich, from one of the wealthiest Latinx families in the country. And she'd always seemed so sad, so quiet. But to him she'd been intriguing, and beautiful. *So damn beautiful.* She brought out his protective instincts like no one outside his mother and sister ever had. He'd been drawn to her from the first moment, and once he'd actually gotten to know her and realized how brilliant and funny she was—he'd fallen hard.

People underestimated Perla, never seeing the fire hiding under those bland clothes and nerdy glasses. She was always so fastidiously put together. She was fine-boned and small, almost waifish, with big gray eyes he'd felt like he could drown in. And she'd dressed to go unnoticed. Pencil skirts and cardigan sets with ballet flats, in every shade of pastel you could imagine. *Cashmere* cardigans, and *designer* skirts and flats, but forgettable, almost old-fashioned. But still, she'd been like a beacon to Gael.

Back then he'd been the big man on campus, at least the part of campus that cared about drama majors and theater. He was poised to be the one star from their graduating class. And once all that potential his teachers kept telling him he had actually turned into acting opportunities, he'd had no idea how to handle it. He'd come from humble beginnings, after all. And almost without warning he'd been thrown into a world of wealth and fame he'd felt lost in. He was tough, a hard worker, and he was no dummy. But he'd needed some insight in how to carry himself in that environment, and Perla had given him all the help he'd needed. She'd taught him where to get his suits and who to go to for a haircut. The right place to rent an apartment in New York City and even what car to drive. She'd been his guide in navigating the world of the one percent, and just when he was poised to soar, he'd left her behind.

He still remembered that night. Could even recall the old Yale sweatshirt he'd been wearing. He could smell the microwave popcorn Perla had made for him that was sitting on her coffee table when he walked into her apartment. After days, weeks of him ignoring his uncle's warnings that his relationship with Perla was hurting his image, it all came to a head when a tabloid plastered a photo of Gael and Perla walking in Manhattan. The headline with the words *Plain Perla* plastered in red had been Manolo's smoking gun. Manolo laid into him about how it was better for everyone to end things. That staying together would be bad for his career and would almost certainly be bad for her mental health. That the media was ruthless, and no matter how hard he tried to protect Perla, her connection to him would end up hurting her. So he'd done it. He cut her out of his life.

Six months after their breakup she'd started popping up in gossip websites and on Page Six, jet-setting around the world. The pastel cardigans all gone and replaced with a bolder, more Instagram-ready version of his shy ex-girlfriend. But once her father died, she seemed to have dropped off the face of the earth. Except now she was on her way to his house. And he wasn't sure how he felt about any of it.

The sound of gravel on his enormous circular driveway jolted his attention back to the present and the car coming toward him. He frowned as a sleek, black Maserati SUV rolled to a stop just a few yards from where he stood. He could feel his forehead scrunching with a frown as he tried to get a closer look at the driver. He'd been expecting a variation on the BMW sedans Perla always drove. Her car choices had always been in line with her modest—for rich people—tastes in fashion. But this was the kind of car you drove to make a statement. He moved closer to it, heart hammering in his chest as he saw the door open.

His plan was to stave Perla off, meet her in the driveway before his mother had a chance to see her, and tell her this was not going to work out. That there was too much baggage for them to be around each other. He moved his feet to reach her car, and even opened his mouth to say it, but once he got a glimpse of her, the words never came. He just stood there, mouth gaping as she slowly opened the door and gave him a full view of the new Perla. This was not the same girl from college or even from those early Instagram posts.

Gone was her usual high ponytail and scrupulously highlighted blond hair. In its place was a raven-black pixie cut that made her big gray eyes sparkle. The winged eyeliner was a surprise, too, and when his eyes drifted down to her mouth, her lips were a cherry red. Perla had never been one to be flashy about her wealth, but if you knew what to look for, you could find it all over her. The vintage Piaget watch on her wrist. The big green Bottega Veneta he recognized from a runway show he'd been dragged to during fashion week.

Everything about Perla Sambrano had always given off old money vibes, but she wore it differently now. There was a boldness to her that hadn't been there before. And she was certainly dressing differently. She had big gold hoops in her ears and the subdued clothing choices of the past were replaced by a black sweater dress and black faux leather leggings. He raised an eyebrow when he noticed the sneakers on her feet. Perla Sambrano in red sneakers. Balenciaga sneakers, but still.

But as she made her way to him, he saw that her outfit and car were not the only things that were different. She threw her head back to put on a pair of oversize sunglasses and when she saw him, the smile on her lips was not the shy expression from the old days. This was the smile of a woman who meant business.

"Gael," she called as she reached him. They were both Latinx, after all, so when she lifted her face to his, he pressed his cheek to hers in hello. His skin tightened as it touched hers and an electric current ran through his limbs. He told himself it must be the chill in the air. That his surprise was the natural reaction to seeing someone after so long. She looked *so different*, he was surprised, that was all. He opened his mouth to say something, anything, then blurted out the one thing that would almost certainly piss her off. "When did you start wearing red lipstick?"

She leaned back like she didn't know what to make of his outburst, then she grinned. The old Perla would've recoiled at his question. In the past, feeling judged had been the fastest way for Perla to clam up. But today she just lifted a shoulder and grinned, cheeky and unfazed by his grumpiness.

"I thought I'd try something new. I got a little tired of neutral." He knew he was glaring, but he didn't seem to be able to come up with words just then. Perla didn't seem to notice his silence. "Thanks for agreeing to do this." She smiled sweetly and something primal pulsed in his chest. Whatever it was, he shut it down immediately.

"Don't thank me. Thank Gabi's pushiness," he groused, sounding harsher than he intended. But Perla's smile deepened at the mention of his sister, unaffected by his surliness.

"Knowing Gabi, I imagine she delivered the news with the subtlety of a freight train," she joked, surprising a laugh out of him. But after a moment a taut silence descended, and they both seemed to run out of pleasantries at the same time. There was no pretending this wasn't awkward. How does anyone handle meeting the person that at one time had meant everything to them? It felt like coming out of a bunker after six years underground and realizing the world had moved on without him. He'd been stagnant, and she'd blossomed.

He'd refused to dwell on his decision to end things after it happened. His whole approach had been to ignore what the breakup did to him. He'd told himself he didn't deserve to mope around when he wasn't the one who got dumped, and he'd put her and everything he lost out of his mind for six years. And that was not something he had any interest in revisiting. Maybe Manolo was right and considering this project was a mistake. He'd only been around Perla for a couple of minutes, and he was already unearthing ancient history.

"Here." He gestured to the steps that led to their house. "Let's go inside and we can talk there."

She nodded, following him. Gael didn't miss that she kept herself a few feet away from him. When it was time to climb the steps to the door, she let him go first and then stood away from him as he pushed it open.

One thing was clear: Perla was here for one thing and one thing only, and that was business.

Three

Perla had been prepared for the cold shoulder. For Gael acting like he'd forgotten who she was, but what she had not been prepared for was the effect Gael Montez's appreciative gaze would have on her. Well, that was a lie—she remembered only too well how being close to him affected her; she'd just hoped time and distance had diluted that vulnerability.

It hadn't.

And if possible, he was even more beautiful now. Larger than life in a way that was…distracting. Gael had always been movie-star handsome. Charisma to spare and the looks to turn heads whenever he walked into the room. People were drawn to him, and he knew how to keep their attention. He'd always been able to command Perla's.

But in six years he'd gone from boyishly hand-some to a rugged, almost dangerous masculinity. He'd always stood nearly a foot taller than she did, but since she'd seen him last he'd gotten bigger, more muscular. All the soft edges gone. He was sporting a beard and had his chin-length hair framing his face. She was not usually into the Winter Soldier look, but Gael pulled it off. He more than pulled it off. God, he could be a Carib warrior with that golden-brown skin, green eyes and chiseled jaw. Yeah, it was for the best that she'd only be here for a couple of hours.

As they made their way up the steps to his impressive home, she caught him sending looks in her direction. Despite her best efforts to remain unbothered, her belly fluttered and a smile tugged up her lips, because she knew what those looks were about. He was intrigued.

In the past year she'd gone for a completely different style. Something that reflected a bit more of her personality. Her whole life she'd taken direction from her mother about everything. From her hair color to the shoes she wore, but she'd freed herself of all that. Perla liked this new version of herself, and from the way Gael kept glomming her up with his eyes, she was thinking he appreciated it, too.

"Here we are," he announced, opening the red door that led to the foyer of the home. It was a stunning place. Built in the Cape Cod style, the exterior was painted in a traditional light blue with white shutters. The interior was modern and with an open floor plan and lots of glass. The better for taking in the gorgeous views of the Long Island Sound.

"This is beautiful," she complimented sincerely as he took her coat. She looked around, admiring the gleaming teak flooring and light gray walls of the foyer. From there she could see the floor-to-ceiling stone fireplace in the living room, which was decorated with garland and tiny white twinkling lights. There was garland everywhere actually, and she expected there would be a huge tree somewhere. Gael's mother had always loved Christmas. Even when they'd lived in their little house in Bridgeport she'd made the space beautiful and festive. Perla was about to ask about his mother when she heard a familiar warm voice call her name.

"Perlita, querida!" Gael shook his head at his mother's exclamation, and Perla couldn't help smiling as she saw the woman come over to her with her arms open wide. Veronica was wearing an old Yale Mom sweatshirt and jeans, her shoulder-length hair now fully white. She looked warm and approachable. The polar opposite of Perla's own mother, who was always groomed to within an inch of her life.

"Doña Veronica," Perla said as she was engulfed into a warm hug. Veronica always smelled like vanilla and warm bread. Perla closed her eyes as the woman cooed over her.

"It's been too long, sweetheart. More than a year now. And what is this Doña business. You call me Veronica, okay?"

Perla smiled at the feigned reproach, but before

she could respond there was a sound from behind her, which she assumed came from Gael. "A year?"

Veronica nodded at her son's comment without taking her eyes off Perla. "Yes, Perlita came to see me after that first surgery. You were in Italy shooting the second Space Squadron."

"Oh."

Perla's face heated at the affronted surprise in Gael's voice, but she wasn't looking up at him. Letting him see her blushing was not advisable. Thankfully, Veronica was not done with her greeting.

"I'm so happy to have you here with us. I love your new style. It suits you." Veronica pulled back to get a better look and smiled down at Perla. It was so good to see her again, but when Perla looked closely, she could see the deep lines around the older woman's eyes. Veronica still had her energy and spark, but Gael's mother had the look of someone who'd just fought a hard battle and won it by the skin of her teeth. "You have to have lunch with us. I want to hear what you've been up to. Gabi said you're working at Sambrano." The older woman paused then and squeezed Perla's hand. "I heard in the news about the changes going on at the studio." Veronica had too many manners to say that she'd seen Perla's family drama plastered all over the news, including how her mother had tried her best to destroy her father's legacy.

"Thank you," Perla said dutifully, not wanting to delve into her still-complicated feelings about her family, her father's death and the mess he'd left for all of them to pick up. He'd been a proud man, hard-working and brilliant, but he'd never been affectionate. He'd given all his children names of gems, but never treated them like they were precious to him. Perla, being the youngest, felt completely invisible to her father. And now that he was gone, realizing she hadn't known her father enough to truly miss him, was almost too painful to dwell on.

"Gael, you need to make sure you're done by lunchtime, so I can visit with Perla!" Veronica's voice brought Perla back to the moment, and she had to smile at the older woman's loving chastisement of her son.

"Sure, Mami."

Perla turned to look at Gael and she saw in the set of his shoulders and the tightness around his mouth that he was looking for any indication that his mother was in pain. He'd always been protective of her. Well, he was protective of everyone; that was one of the many reasons Perla had fallen fast and hard for Gael. But his mother had always been his main priority. Perla never had the unconditional love Gael had always received from his mother, but she knew the responsibility he felt for taking care of the woman who raised him. Gael was a man who never shied from his duty. He always did what it took to take care of his people. She'd loved that about him…and that was *not* where her head needed to be at all.

"We should get going. I have a flight later today and need to be on the road in a couple of hours," she said tersely.

"Sure." Gael nodded, giving her a questioning look. But whatever he was wondering about, he didn't ask it. After letting her say a quick goodbye to his mother he briskly led her through the living room, which indeed had an enormous tree in the corner. They walked by framed windows showcasing an awe-inspiring view of the ocean, and walls lined with family photographs and quite a few pieces of art.

Unlike her own mother's house, which looked like a Versace home showroom, Veronica's house was furnished for comfort. Dozens of photos of Gael, Gabi and Veronica and other family members hanging on the walls or in frames on practically every surface. The brown leather sectional looked inviting, like it could easily sit half a dozen people. There were also armchairs and ottomans scattered around the room. All of them looked well used. The Montez home was a place for family. In the past she'd yearned to be one of them. To belong to these people who loved each other so deeply, but Gael had not seen her as his forever.

"This is very nice, Gael." She knew buying a home in the Hamptons for his mother was one of his dreams. When they'd been together, he told her that when he was in middle school his mom worked as a housekeeper for a wealthy family in Southampton during the summer. The estate had a small apartment over the stable and she would bring Gael and Gabi with her. He told Perla he'd loved and hated those summers. Loved the beautiful coast and playing on the beach with his sister but hated how the family treated his mother. He'd confessed to Perla that one night after he'd seen his mom almost pass out from exhaustion, he'd promised himself that one day he would be rich and buy her one of those big houses… and he had. She wanted to ask him if he remembered telling her that. Instead, she turned around, admiring the room in silence, until she trusted herself to speak. "Your mother must be very pleased."

He made a noise that was more of a groan than a yes and stopped right as they reached the fireplace, which was blazing happily. "You know how she is." He smiled wryly and looked around the big room with the ten-million-dollar view he'd bought for his mother. "It took six months to convince her we needed a decorator to help her."

"I can imagine." Perla smiled knowingly as she admired the room. Gael's mother would probably not be one to think spending money on something as frivolous as a decorator was necessary.

"Come," he said, breaking the tense silence between them. "We can do the reading in the study." He laughed awkwardly as he opened the door to the massive room. "I'm not sure what else to call it."

"Wow, this is amazing," Perla said in a reverent whisper as she followed him to the doorway and took in the rows and rows of books along the walls. Like in the living room, there was a blazing fire here, and there was an ocean view, too. But what captured her attention were the bookshelves and the enormous screen in the far end. There were four brown leather armchairs in a semicircle in front of a screen that wouldn't have been out of place in a movie house. She turned to look at the other end of the room where there was a love seat and a Herman Miller chair, presumably for reading. This place was for two things: books and movies.

Gael's—*and Perla's*—two favorite things.

Dissecting books and movies they both loved had been one of the ways they'd bonded when they first became friends. Later, when they'd been much more than that, their shared passion had been one of the things that convinced Perla they were perfect for each other. That despite their outward differences in background and even personality, at the core they were kindred spirits. And she absolutely had to stop reminiscing; she was already on a slippery slope as it was.

Forcing herself to shake off the maudlin thoughts flooding her, she stepped into the large room. The walls were covered in a midnight blue wallpaper with little flecks of gold. The effect almost gave the sensation of being surrounded by a starry night sky. The dark wood of the built-in bookshelves and warm lighting made it cozy and inviting. It was a room for slowing down and doing the things you enjoyed. She had her own version of it in her apartment on the Upper West Side of Manhattan.

"Come over here," Gael called, piercing through her thoughts. She turned her head to find him standing by the bookshelves. He was pointing at one of them, presumably for her to look at, but her eyes kept wanting to drift over him. He was dressed simply, in

black joggers and hoodie, and he still looked imposing. Those wide shoulders tapering down to a trim
waist. His powerful thighs stretching the fabric of
his pants so that she could almost see the outline of
his muscles. He was so intensely male. It was hard
not to stare at that powerful, virile body.

"I think you'll get a kick out of these." Again, his
voice startled her.

"Sorry," she told him as she came closer. "I got
distracted." He gave her a long look, but didn't comment on her obvious flustered state.

Once she was close enough, she leaned in to scan
the shelf and gasped as she saw the titles of all of Gabriel García Márquez's books. The Nobel Laureate
was Perla's favorite author, and it seemed like Gael
had collected *all* of his books. "Are these first editions?" she asked, feeling a little dazed. She owned a
few herself, but some of the titles he had were practically impossible to find.

"They are." He sounded more than a little pleased
with himself. And she would not be foolish enough
to think this man was attempting to impress her.
"You might also like what I have in the next shelf."
She turned and squealed with delight to find rows
and rows of romance novels. Also her favorite, and
something she'd gotten Gael into in college. She'd
talked him into trying them by saying he could learn
about capturing the inner life of the characters, especially the heroes in the stories. She'd told him romance authors wrote big emotions like no one else,
and it would help him when he needed to get into a

character's head. Gael hadn't been too convinced, but he'd read them—he was always willing to try anything that would help him be better at his job. It didn't take long for him to get hooked on them and soon they were swapping books.

Suddenly feeling a bit overwhelmed, Perla forced herself to straighten and step back from the old editions of Johanna Lindsey books, and turned to Gael.

"This is a lovely collection," she said coolly, needing to keep herself at a distance. "But let's talk business." She forced herself to offer him a smile as she tried to shake her nerves off. "I know you probably want me out of your hair." She didn't wait for an answer and launched into her pitch for the show. She talked rapidly as she pulled out the full script from her bag. "I know you're interested in this role," she told him in a tone that brooked no argument. He just leaned into the bookshelf, a neutral look on his face. "This is a special project," she said, confidently. "Caballero-Mendez came to us asking to write the screenplay."

He arched an eyebrow at that, interest edging out his feigned indifference. Good call, Gabi. "Everyone involved in this project is an all-star. This project could cement your versatility as an actor." Perla mentally patted herself on the back for managing to deliver that with a lot more confidence than she felt.

He eyed her from his stance a few feet away as if he was trying to read something on her face. Her skin heated from the intensity of his stare, and just when she was about to break, he finally spoke.

"I'm surprised you're working for Sambrano." That was not where she expected the conversation to go. Even if the comment was fair enough. Back when they'd been together, Perla never wasted an opportunity to affirm she had no interest in working for her father's company.

"My family owns the studio," she hedged and in response he arched an eyebrow that said *That's always been the case.* She raised a shoulder, as if she was bored with the conversation, buying herself time to come up with an answer. "My sister's the president now, and…" She trailed off, not wanting to get into this with Gael. She'd always had a tendency to spill her feelings whenever he was around.

"You never had an interest in working for your father *or* the company."

"That was a long time ago, Gael." She was going to say, *You have no idea about what I'm interested in*, but she decided that antagonizing him was not the way to go, and before she knew it, she was telling him the truth. "My sister's a very different leader than my father was, and she wants me there, views me as an asset. And you know what else?" She crossed her arms in an identical gesture to his. "I believe in the vision she has for the studio."

"You've really changed," he said, and she almost bristled. But his tone wasn't judgmental or sharp. It was almost like he was thinking aloud. Putting things together.

"I have," she confirmed, unable to keep the challenge out of her voice.

He stared at her again in that unnerving way he'd been doing since they'd come into the room. After a moment he shook himself and grabbed the script from where she'd put it on the love seat.

"All right, then. Let's see what magic Caballero-Mendez did with this script." With that he came to stand barely a foot away from her and opened the binder to a scene in the middle of the screenplay. "Read with me."

Four

This was what he got from trying to be all cavalier.
A fucking disaster.

"I don't think this scene is a good idea," Gael said
through gritted teeth, while Perla looked at him with
angelic eyes. He'd been surprised by the calm and
steady way in which she talked about her work and
her family. This version of Perla was so different
than the girl he'd fallen in love with. He felt thrown
by her presence and whenever Gael felt unsteady, he
was impulsive. And now he'd impulsed himself into
doing a kissing scene with Perla Sambrano. Who
seemed not only unbothered, but kind of amused
about his little freak-out.

"Lighten up, Gael. It's just a kiss. You're a professional, and I didn't think you'd forget that I was an

arts major, too. I can handle a fake kiss. Believe me, I know it's not going to be the real thing."

She was goading him. He looked down at her as she stood there, her face fixed in an expression of absolute calm. The only thing that betrayed the little game she was playing was the barely visible tremor on her top lip. She was nervous, too.

"So you're cool about us kissing, then? No big deal?" The skin on his face tightening as adrenaline roared through his veins. She wanted to pretend, to play like this wasn't getting to her. He was going to call her bluff.

"Yep." She nodded and again he almost missed that her smile was just on this side of panicked.

"All right, then," he said, voice like gravel from the sudden pulsing in his groin. And that was so unprofessional. What was going on with him? He was better than this. He was an experienced actor; he knew how to keep himself in check in intimate scenes, had done them hundreds of times. But the prospect of a kiss with Perla had beads of sweat dripping down his back. This was a stupid, reckless idea. He should just end this. Tell Perla he knew she was bluffing. That this little game she was playing to get back at him for the way things ended between them was not going anywhere.

The Perla he'd known would've never pulled something petty like this. If he had any sense at all he'd back off from this whole thing, tell her he wasn't going to take the part. That Gabi misjudged his level of interest. That was the *sane* thing to do, but he didn't do any of it. Instead, he took a step closer, his hand crushing the script, and his gaze fixed on Perla's cherry-red lips.

"Ready?" She gave one terse nod and moved within kissing range.

The scene was the moment when Francisco Rios and Claudia Mieses kissed for the first time. They were supposed to be walking in Cambridge late at night. It was fall and a little chilly. Claudia was shivering, and Francisco stopped and embraced her, then he kissed her.

"Tienes frío," he said, following the lines as he gathered her in his arms. Perla looked surprised that he'd started without warning, but soon she went with it. She glanced up at him, and there was something in her eyes he could not quite read. Something he'd never seen before. A fiery, challenging gaze that came with this more brazen version of Perla.

"Francisco, kiss me," she pleaded. And there was a tremor in her voice, like she could barely control the urgency, the need for his touch. The words ignited something hot and wild in him, even as he reminded himself she was only reading her lines. That the trembling in her voice was just acting.

That it was all fake.

He strived to clear his head as he pressed closer. Tried desperately to find his focus, to channel what he needed to convey. His heart was punching into the walls of his chest as he bent his head to reach her mouth. Those full red lips were beckoning to him, and it was useless telling himself this was like any other kiss on a set. Perla was a full assault on his senses. The curves of her, her pert breasts pressed to his chest, her warm softness brushing against him, set him on fire.

Focus, Gael. Focus. You are Francisco and this is Claudia. There's no history and no baggage here. Just two actors infusing themselves into their roles.

He ran his finger across Perla's hairline. Francisco was supposed to tug on an errant curl on Claudia's forehead, but Perla's short hair didn't allow for that. She sighed when he touched her and he bent down, his eyes wide open, taking her in. She was so beautiful, he'd always known that, but now it wasn't just some piece of information he stored to never examine again. It was a palpable, undeniable fact. From the notes, he knew this scene took place after Francisco and Claudia had been dancing around each other for months. That they'd been resisting the growing, undeniable attraction between them until this moment. The prelude to this kiss was the final instant before they tore down the last wall and took their friendship to a new place. A place that would lead to an epic love story, to marriage, children. It was a kiss that would change the course of their lives. And when his lips finally crashed onto Perla's and she melted against him, tightening her slender arms around his neck, Gael tossed out any attempt at pretending this was an act.

Perla had forced herself to not think about Gael's kisses for the past six years. Had told herself again and again that the breakup had been for the best. That she was not cut out for life in the spotlight. That she was too much of an introvert, and he was too gregarious for them to ever work long-term. That even if it had hurt like hell, Gael had been right, that *they* weren't right. She'd drilled into her head that his kisses weren't perfect. That his arms hadn't been the one place in the world where she felt safe.

She'd been deluding herself.

Just a moment in the man's arms and she knew if she didn't pull away, she'd be ruined. Gael's grunt of pleasure as their lips met was a deep, possessive sound, and in an instant she was lost to him. She bit on his bottom lip and her tongue went exploring. That elicited another satisfied groan, and soon they were devouring each other. The thought occurred to her that for all that they were different, one thing remained very much the same: he was still the only man she'd completely given herself to.

She'd made up endless excuses for why that was still the case. That she needed more time, that she had trust issues…but it was all nonsense, because the real reason was that she'd fallen for the wrong man and she'd never gotten over him. And that man was currently ravishing her mouth like he wanted to consume her.

He was acting, she told herself as lust threatened to edge out every sensible thought in her head. This wasn't Gael, who had finally realized that Perla had been the one all along. That they were perfect for each other. No, this was an actor doing his job. Performing, pretending that he was burning up for the woman in his arms. This was Francisco Rios kissing Claudia Mieses. In a minute, less than that, they would pull back. Their bodies would unlock from this searing embrace, she'd politely thank Gael for considering the role and she would get in her car and drive away.

That was what had to happen. Perla wasn't foolish enough to think this was anything other than a job for Gael. But it was hard to be sensible when her tongue was sensuously sliding against his, and his big, rough hands gripped her like he would never let her go. The scruff of his beard grazing against her cheek electrified her, and his rosemary-and-mint shampoo was all she could smell. She was wrapped up in Gael again, just like she'd dreamed a thousand times.

Somewhere in the recesses of her mind, Perla thought she heard a door open, that she sensed footsteps on one of the Serapi rugs in the room. She wondered if she should tell Gael, but his lips were on her neck and his hands were on her backside, and she would do almost anything to stay just like this for a second longer. No matter what she'd told herself on the drive here and no matter what she would most likely lecture herself with for the rest of her life, this moment was too good to cut short.

"Yo lo sabía!" Veronica's delighted voice broke the spell, causing Perla to practically fly out of Gael's arms.

"I told Gabi you two had finally seen the light.

I've been praying for this for years." Perla didn't even know where to look. She'd never had much luck when it came to public humiliation, and it seemed her streak of doom was not done yet. Gael's mother approached Perla with what, to her utter horror, looked very much like tears in her eyes, and gave her a strong hug, which she helplessly reciprocated. She had no idea what to do or say, and hoped that Gael would react at some point and tell his mother what was actually going on. But Veronica was in the throes of euphoria.

"You two are just so perfect for each other," Veronica exclaimed. "I've been telling him for six years he made the biggest mistake of his life when he let you go. I've never seen my baby happier than when you two—"

"Ma! Por favor," Gael called from whichever corner of the room he'd run off to when he'd been caught with both hands on Perla's ass and his mouth on her neck.

"I'm just happy for you, mijo." Veronica raised her gaze in her son's direction, her radiant smile still firmly in place.

This was brutal.

Perla had always known Gael's mother cared for her. The woman had welcomed her into their home from that first time she came to visit with Gabi after they'd ended up in the same dorm. With the Montez family Perla had finally understood what it meant to feel like you belonged. They always acted like she was not just welcome, but that she was also expected.

And now seeing the real joy in Veronica's face at the idea that she and Gael were an item again...it was like getting punched in the stomach.

Because the one thing she would not let herself dwell on were the "what-ifs" when it came to Gael. Seeing Veronica's reaction, her words, it was too painful, and dammit, she was not going to fix this. Gael was the one who pushed that kiss, who touched her like he wanted her, who made her forget herself. He had to fix this now.

"It's just been so long since I saw you happy, Gael. You two together, it's my Christmas miracle." Veronica let her out of the embrace but kept her hand firmly in Perla's, like she couldn't stand to let this moment slip away.

"Mami," Gael groaned, his gaze fixed in the far distance like there was something there he desperately wanted to reach—probably his patience. "This is not what you think. Perla and I—"

He paused, his mouth in a hard line. And things between them hadn't been over so long Perla couldn't see that Gael was trying to get himself under control. His mother would see it, too, but Veronica waited him out. Like if she gave him enough time he'd realize she was right about what she'd seen.

Finally, after what seemed like hours, Gael looked at Perla and then at his mother, his eyes boring in on whatever he saw on the older woman's face. His expression was unreadable. He walked over to them, focused on his mother, and Perla braced herself for when he would finally put all this to rest. When he let his mother know she'd misread the situation.

But instead, he reached for Perla, and with a fake smile tugging up his lips, he opened his gorgeous mouth and lied his face off.

Five

Perla was stiff as a board in his arms, and he couldn't blame her. He'd just told his mother that they were back together. He didn't dare look down at his fake significant other, because she was probably ready to murder him. And he *had been* intending to come clean, but when he saw the tears of joy in his mother's eyes, he hadn't been able to do it. This was the happiest he'd seen her since she got really sick last year. She'd been giddy to find them necking in the study, and he would be damned if he took that from this woman after the hell she'd been through.

"We just didn't want to tell you until I was back home. You know how it is, better to give the news in person." He lied to the woman who brought him into the world as he put an arm around the woman who was most likely plotting how to take him out of it, if the murder noises Perla was making were any indication.

"Of course I understand! This kind of news is best given in person!" his mother exclaimed with a knowing wink as she leaned in to kiss him on the cheek, and then moved in to give another hug to Perla, who was looking a little pale. "You wanted to have Perlita here when you told us. Querida," his mother said, turning to his supposed girlfriend, who so far had not uttered a single word. "I'm so glad we get you for a little visit, but can you stay a little longer?"

That request seemed to finally snap Perla out of her shock. "I have to catch my flight, Veronica. I can't stay very long."

The frown on Gael's mother's face was the one that usually came before emotional extortion a la Latin mom ensued. "Ay pero, just for a little bit. We want to see you, too, and this muchacho has kept you all to himself since you got here. I knew you couldn't really be here for work. It's Christmas! And since you can't be with us for Nochebuena we have to get some quality time with you." Her eyes widened as if she'd just had a great idea. "We just made alcapurrias this morning. I can fry some up for you! You used to love them."

Gael could tell that she was about to throw in the towel, and who could blame her? Veronica Montez could always wield a hard bargain with her culinary offerings.

"I still do," Perla said, admitting defeat.

"Great!" His mother was giddy. "Just give me ten minutes, okay?" Without waiting for an answer, his mother flew out of the room completely unaware of the fiasco currently unfolding.

"You are *unbelievable*," Perla accused as she stepped out from under his arm.

"What's so unbelievable about me not wanting to break my mother's heart during the holidays?" Gael knew he was being an unreasonable bastard, but in the past few minutes, keeping this lie going had turned into his one mission in life. "Not that this is your problem, but she almost died, Perla. I managed to keep it out of the tabloids but that one surgery she had ended up being like five surgeries, and after the last one we didn't think she'd walk again. This is the first time I've seen her really smile in almost six months." Perla's face crumpled at that, and he saw when his words began to edge out her annoyance at him. "I know I don't have any right to ask you for this, but it's going to be an hour maybe two of pretending we're seeing each other."

"I don't like lies," she protested weakly, her gaze on the door his mother had practically skipped out of earlier.

"I know." He rubbed his face hard with the palm of his hand. "This is a lot to ask. But you'll be out of here and on the way to the airport after lunch," he reminded her. "After the holidays and once things have calmed down a bit, I'll tell her that we couldn't make the long-distance thing work."

"I don't know, Gael," she said nervously. He was

aware this was not a small concession. He also knew Perla had made the trip over here for a reason. He had something she wanted, something she'd been willing to do despite their history and the baggage she'd be dragging back to the surface, and he was enough of a bastard to use it.

"I'll take the role," he offered, before he could talk himself out of it. He had to suppress a smile at the way she perked up. If she had antennae they'd be twitching on top of her head. Yeah, people saw Perla Sambrano, the pampered rich girl, and they had no idea there was a driven, fierce perfectionist under all that. Perla liked to be good at things, and she liked to make the people she loved proud of her; she liked to make them happy. If her sister wanted this, Perla would do whatever it took to deliver it.

"You'll commit knowing virtually nothing about the terms of the project in exchange for me pretending that we're dating for the duration of a meal?" She sounded irritated, which made his dick pulse in his sweats. She was so sexy like this, with that hint of bloodthirst in her eyes.

"You informed me earlier that all I needed to know was that I'd be a fool not to be a part of this project."

"True." She flashed a little smart-ass grin at that, and he almost scooped her clear off the floor and kissed her senseless, but the priority was his mother. He had to stay on task.

"You know I'd do anything for my mother, Perla. I realize you don't think much of me." He put both his hands up in a conciliatory gesture when her gray eyes narrowed to slits. "You have good reason to hate me, but I at least hope you could remember that."

"I don't hate—" She started to protest, but whatever she saw in his expression made her close her mouth.

She turned her face up to him. He towered over her by almost a foot, which meant that she had to turn her head almost ninety degrees to face him and something primitive in him reveled in that.

"I go out there and pretend we're dating, have lunch with your family, then leave and you will play Francisco Rios in our series?" she asked.

Gael nodded, his arms crossed on his chest to curb the insane urge to pull her to him.

"And you break the news to her afterward. I won't be expected to pretend later, and you won't make me the bad guy in any of this."

"Correct," he confirmed through gritted teeth, and he wanted to rip out the swarm of bees that had taken residence in his chest. Blood rushed to his ears as he waited for her answer.

Her eyebrows almost came together as she considered his words, clearly trying to figure out where the catch was, but after a moment her arms dropped to her sides and she exhaled, gaze still locked on his. "Fine, two alcapurrias and I'm out of here."

She stormed out of the room in a cloud of black and cherry red and he stayed rooted in place watching her pert little ass as she made her way to his mother's kitchen.

* * *

"Perla!" The welcoming choir from the kitchen put a smile on Perla's face despite how out of sorts she was feeling.

"Come give me a hug, niña," Gael's grandmother demanded as she turned golden-brown empanadas in a pot of bubbling hot oil.

"Doña Juana," Perla said as she put an arm around the small woman.

"Call me Abuela, querida, and especially now that my grandson has finally wised up and gotten you back." The older woman carefully plucked the last of the empanadas out of the oil as she talked and turned off the gas, then turned around to wrap Perla into a fierce hug. The roughened palm patting her cheek with such tender affection had tears prickling her eyes.

"I'm so happy you're here. Now get those empanadas and put them on the table. Then we can talk about your new look. Gaelito can't keep his eyes off you," Juana teased and Perla looked up to find the Hollywood actor in question leaning against the arch that led from the kitchen to the dining room. The house had enough square footage to easily accommodate a dozen people, just in the kitchen, so Perla hadn't noticed Gael walking in. And he *was* looking at her, very intensely looking at her. He was too damn fine for words, and she really, really wished he'd stop being this damn sexy all the time.

"Here, let me help you," he said, pushing off the wall. He picked up the plate of empanadas and she followed him into the next room. She imagined all that sinew and muscle she'd gripped and felt against her when they kissed, shifting and flexing as he moved. Her lips were still bruised from the kiss, and Perla couldn't help sliding her tongue over the spot on her bottom lip where he'd sucked on it. He must've noticed the gesture because he froze for a second and a flush of heat spread through her just from that. She had to turn around and occupy herself with the task of arranging the food on a dish to keep from doing something supremely stupid.

Even looking at the man was dangerous.

With every word exchanged, every touch, feelings and yearnings she'd hoped had been buried and dead long ago cropped up like crocuses announcing the end of a long, dark winter. But she could do this; it was only two hours. Veronica would have her Christmas without drama, and Perla would deliver Gael Montez for *The Liberator and His Love*. All she had to do was keep her head in the game. If there was something Perla knew how to do it was repress every emotion. To pretend nothing was wrong, even when she could barely hold it together. Her mother had made sure her children could always present a happy face, no matter how miserable they felt. She was a pro at "fake it till you make it" and she would not falter in this. One meal with Gael and his family. Then she'd drive away and call her sister with the good news.

She needed this win. Not because Esmeralda was

putting pressure on her, but because she wanted to prove to herself she could see this through.

All she had to do to fulfill her end of the bargain was pretend for a little bit. She didn't like lying to Veronica—she was sure Gael wasn't thrilled about it either, but he'd do what he needed to, in order to make his mother happy. In college she'd found it utterly disarming that the rough, brilliant, beautiful boy who seemed to have every girl on campus dying to be on his arm, would leave New Haven every Saturday afternoon and make his way down to Bridgeport so he could see his mother. One of the many things about Gael that had made her fall hard.

"Mami, I'm back!"

Gabi's voice pierced through Perla's musings. She should've assumed Gael's sister would make an appearance, but the past twenty minutes had been so chaotic she hadn't had time to think about who else they'd have to involve in this farce. Gabi would not buy that they were dating. First, Gael told his sister everything, and second, Gabi knew exactly why she was here. And as good an actor as her brother was, Gabi did not have a poker face. Perla turned from the platter of empanadas she was pretending to arrange and put her arms around Gael's neck. Her mouth barely reached his throat, so she had to rise on her tiptoes to speak close to his ear.

She wished that he didn't feel this good. That the reality of him didn't make every one of her many fantasies pale in comparison. A wicked and not a little bit reckless thought occurred to her as they stood there pressed together in his family's dining room: she had the next couple of hours to touch Gael Montez as much as she wanted.

It would be a problem later; she knew that. She was already halfway back to that emotional chaos that only Gael could cause in her, but she found that she didn't much care. How could she deny herself this feast of a man when he was literally offering himself up on a silver platter? Was it reckless? Yes. But he'd asked her to pretend. No, not asked, demanded. He'd demanded she play this role for the next two hours. The role of besotted girlfriend, that they convince his mother they were an item once again. And that was how they'd been back then. Constantly touching, Veronica, Gabi and Abuela had mercilessly teased them about "all the PDA."

"What are you doing?" he asked tersely, without pulling back.

"Did you tell Gabi?" Immediately he tightened his arms around her. His massive chest like a living, breathing wall against her.

He nodded before he opened his mouth and the way his scruff grazed against her skin made shivers course all through her body. "Gabi knows. I caught her before she went to take the dogs out."

"Okay," Perla answered in a breathy tone, her lips brushing the side of his neck. She smiled at the strangled noise that came out of him in response. Something between a growl and a groan, and almost instantly he moved them until she had her back against the wall.

"If you're trying to play games with me, don't," he gritted out, his big body pressed to her. "I will call your bluff, every time, Perla. I thought you'd know that by now. Or was that kiss in the study not enough of a warning for you?"

She didn't know why she was provoking him. But her better judgment seemed to be on permanent hiatus when it came to Gael Montez. And there was something else she was testing. Another motive behind her urge to push him. She was trying to answer the question she'd been asking herself for six years. How had Gael gone from being devoted to her to heartlessly indifferent practically overnight?

She'd never quite figured out where things had gone so wrong with them. Because Gael had never given her reason to doubt his devotion to her. Then without explanation he'd let her go. Now that she was with him, that she could touch him and feel his reaction to her, it was beyond her to not find out if she still had that effect on him.

She tipped her face up so that her lips were just inches from his. "And here I was thinking that was just how you kissed on all your auditions."

He scowled at that, biting his bottom lip, like he had no idea what to do with her. "What's going on with you, Perla? You're not like this." He sounded confused, and something else that she could not quite pinpoint. Annoyed or not, his arms enveloped her and she felt a shiver course through his body as he held her. Still, that he saw her as some frail waif nettled.

"You haven't known what I'm like for a very long time, Gael," she retorted, sliding from under the cage he'd made with his body. "And what could possibly be going on with me? Other than having to lie to your whole family."

The meal was wonderful. The food delicious and full of all her favorite Puerto Rican treats. The kind of stuff her mother had never served when they were kids, but that her grandmother would make whenever she'd come for a visit from the DR. But it wasn't just the food, it was the company. She'd grown up in a home where there wasn't much warmth. Perla's parents had a toxic, tempestuous relationship that sucked the joy out of every moment. Which was why her time with the Montez family had been such a balm. People who sat around the table and talked. Laughed with each other, *liked* each other.

She'd told herself the whole ordeal would be agonizing, that Gael would be awkward and that she'd be flustered counting the minutes until it was over. But she could not have been more wrong. The moment they'd all sat down, it felt like the old days. Like one of the many weekends when Perla had driven down with Gael for a meal. Forgone a fancy weekend somewhere with her own family to be with the Montez crew. No matter what she might have told herself, she'd missed these people; she'd missed him.

"It's been so nice to have you with us, Perlita," Veronica said for what had to be the tenth time since they'd sat down to eat. All through the meal she'd been getting sly smiles from Abuela and Veronica as if they'd approved of her and Gael getting all handsy in the dining room. "You have to come and spend some time with us after you get back from Punta Cana. You know you can come here even if this boy is off on location, doing all that fancy stuff he does."

"I will," she lied, reaching for her glass of water. Her gaze fixed on one of the wreaths stamped all over the tablecloth.

"I'm so sad you have to rush off," Gabi said and Perla almost believed she was being sincere.

"Perla has to go to the airport," Gael protested, and even though it really shouldn't, it still hurt that he seemed in such a rush to get her out of his hair. And she *should* be heading out. She had been looking forward to spending time with Esmeralda and Rodrigo. Esme's mother and tias had been warm and welcoming on the few occasions Perla had met them. But it wouldn't be like it was with these people, who had always let her be herself. She repressed the sigh in her chest and looked around the table one more time. Steeling herself for the "see you soons" that were coming when she knew there would be no visits or times with Gael and his family ever again.

"But her flight isn't until late tonight and it's not even 3:00 p.m.," Abuela argued. "You still have a little time," the adorable, wily older woman said in that way that made it impossible to deny her anything. "Come down to the basement kitchen with us to help make the pasteles de yuca for a little bit and *then* go," Abuela suggested, knowing Perla had a weakness for pasteles. "I need to get some information about *La Venganza*. These cliffhangers are killing me and I know you have the scoop!" Perla laughed at the reference of the very popular telenovela being aired on one of Sambrano's networks.

"That's confidential information, Abuela," she said with a smile as she stood up, helping clear the plates.

"Mama's right, Gael. She can come down and help us for a bit. That way we can send you with some for your sister," Veronica cajoled, making Perla thaw a little more to the idea of sticking around. She *could* stay a little longer.

Without looking at Gael—and encountering his most likely disapproving expression—Perla conceded. "Abuela's pasteles are very hard to resist. Are you going to help us, babe?" she asked Gael sweetly. She knew at this point she was poking the angry bear, but hey, he had started this fiasco so he was going to suffer with her.

He pasted on a smile so fake she was tempted to ask if that was the best he could do for the millions he got per film. But when he reached for his mom, and kissed the top of her head then whispered an earnest, "Whatever makes you happy, Mami," Perla melted into a puddle before following their lead downstairs, ready to take part in the Montez family Christmas tradition.

Six

"Pass me the filling, querida," Gael's mother asked Perla, and his pretend girlfriend promptly picked up the bowl of shredded pork and handed it over without missing a beat. It was like time hadn't passed at all. Perla had been folded into his family like she'd never left.

The most irritating part of all was that he kept forgetting none of this was real.

For the past hour they'd all been making the pasteles. Every year his family made a few dozen of the Caribbean version of tamales to give to relatives and enjoy as part of their Nochebuena dinner. Even when his mom had been struggling to keep a roof over their heads, working three jobs to make ends meet, she'd somehow managed to get the stuff to make a few pasteles. In those lean years they'd eaten a rotisserie chicken instead of a pernil, and the arroz con gandules had only been enough for one serving each. But their mom would set the table like they were having a lavish meal. She made sure there were a few small gifts to open on Christmas Day.

Gael sometimes was a little numb to his career success. Once the opportunities finally started coming in, it seemed like he could barely keep up with the demands, much less enjoy what he already had. Then there were these moments. Getting to watch his mother and grandmother make pasteles in one of the two big kitchens of the mansion he'd bought. He was proud of this.

And almost as if she'd been reading his mind, Perla opened her mouth. "I'm so glad I got to see the house with all the Christmas decor up."

His mother smiled, looking up from wrapping a pastel in banana leaves. "Gael likes to spoil the people he loves. Don't you, mijo?"

"You deserve it," he muttered huskily, and felt Perla's eyes boring into his side. She'd always done that, been able to see more than anyone else. But this was not the time to dwell on the past. All of that was water under the bridge. One of the many sacrifices he'd made along the way in order to make sure his career thrived. In order to make sure his mother never went without ever again.

He just needed to keep it together a little longer and things would be back to normal. Continuing to be in the same room with Perla when everyone expected them to touch was flirting with disaster; that was a fact. But they were on the home stretch. His mother got her QT with Perla and now it was time for her to go, and if something hot and angry pulsed in his chest at the idea of her leaving, then that was to be dealt with later.

"Tell me about your new job, Perlita?" Veronica asked, and even though Gael kept his eyes on the batter he was spooning, his attention was on what Perla would say.

"I'm doing all the talent acquisitions for the studio's bigger projects and overseeing all our casting departments." He could hear the excitement in her voice, and despite this shit show the two of them had started, he was glad for her. "My sister, Esmeralda, and her fiancé, Rodrigo, have been at the helm for a year now and they're both very invested in bringing back the kind of programming the studio had at the start. More shows that reflect all the faces of Latin America. Our mission is to show as much as we possibly can of the seven hundred million people who are part of the Latinx world."

Gael's abuela made a sound of approval at Perla's words. "That's good, mija. I noticed that the shows weren't the same. I remember that Sambrano was the first network to have a Black Puerto Rican couple as protagonists in a telenovela. That made me a fan for life, but in the past few years it's been different."

Gael looked at Perla then, wondering what her reaction would be to his grandmother's comment. He found her giving the older woman an apologetic smile. "You're right, Abuela. We lost our way for a while there, but we're determined to bring the network back to that mission. I'm proud to be part of the effort."

Before Gael could stop himself he opened his mouth, "You're really enjoying the work, then."

Perla gave him a baleful look. "I do enjoy it, and I'm even good at it." The look she gave him, like she expected him to say something dismissive, cut a bit, but he guessed he deserved it.

"I don't doubt it. You're brilliant," he told her. It wasn't like it was a lie. God, his head was a mess; too many feelings that he did not want to be cropping up were practically flooding him. The longer he was with her the worse it would get. And he knew where it would all end, badly, just like it had before. It was time to end this.

"It's almost 4:00. You said you wanted to be on the road before it got totally dark." He sounded like an ogre, but there was no helping it.

"Sure." Perla nodded, looking hurt. And dammit, it was not his job to keep Perla Sambrano happy no matter how much he ached to see that frown on her face disappear. "Darn, I must've left my phone in my bag upstairs," she said as she rinsed her hands. "I'm supposed to check in with the crew at the airport in case there are any issues. It was so good to visit with you all." She moved around the basement kitchen island and put her arm around Veronica, but his mother shook her head.

"No, we'll go up with you. We have to see you

off properly. Mami's getting some pasteles packed up for you." Within seconds they were all walking up to the main floor of the house and that was when Gael noticed the sound of the wind. A glance out the window confirmed that the gusts were intense and snow was coming down hard. He could barely see anything, the usual view of sky and sea completely blurred out by the heavy snow.

"Oh, no," Gabi said ominously. "Perla, you can't drive out in that."

"But I have my flight," she declared as she warily looked out the window.

"You cannot go out in this, Perla." It wasn't a command, but just barely.

He had to shove his fists in his pockets to keep from grabbing her when she made a move for the door like she was actually planning to drive in that blizzard. Gael could see his mother furrowing her brow, too. And he knew it was only a matter of seconds before she suggested Perla stay with them until the weather improved. And yeah, that would be a major disaster, but he wasn't going to risk her getting into an accident.

"Sure I can," she told him, like he was overreacting. "The SUV has all-wheel drive." With every word out of her mouth Gael had a harder time not forbidding her to leave the house, especially when she kept putting on layers like she was going somewhere. "I bet it's just a squall. I'll probably drive right out of it once I'm farther from the coast," she assured them as she plucked her purse from the couch and set it on the floor by the door. "Here, let me check my messages." She was only in her socks, but had pulled out her sneakers from the rack by the door. The urge to grab her and keep her safely in his house until the snow stopped was so intense he was practically levitating.

If she stayed, she would stay there as his girlfriend, and these past two hours had already frayed his nerves raw. He didn't give a damn. All he cared about was keeping her safe.

"Shoot."

The tension in his neck and shoulders barely allowed him to snap his head back in her direction. He could hear the edge of panic in her voice as she read through whatever was on her phone. She squeezed her eyes shut for a moment and before she opened her mouth, he knew what she'd say. "The flight's canceled until noon tomorrow at least. The crew from the jet said they can't be cleared for take-off because there's a weather system coming through over the next eighteen hours."

He was still considering why his chest was tight enough to suffocate him, when his mother's scream of delight broke through the tension in the room.

"Well, you can just stay here! And if the flight can't go out tomorrow, you'll celebrate Nochebuena with us. I'm sure your sister will want you to stay put until it's safe to fly again." Gael's lips tugged up a little at how pleased his mother looked. Even if this was definitely a terrible turn of events.

Perla kept sending him looks that practically

screamed "This is all your fault," and maybe it was, but he certainly was not sending her out in these conditions. They would just have to extend their fake relationship for a little longer, and that was that.

"Mami, take it easy on poor Perla," he said, trying very hard to sound at ease as he made his way to her. "You're going to scare her off. Give me your keys," he said, extending out his hand to her. "I'll get your bag for you."

"My bag?" she asked, like she had no idea what the word meant.

"*Your bag*, so you can have your stuff for tonight." He kept his hand out while she glared at him and the rest of his family looked on. He knew his mother was poised to go into full-on mama bear mode as soon as Perla relented.

Perla looked up at him, her face defiant, and moved in until she could bring his head down low enough for her to talk into his ear. She wrapped her arms around his neck and he thought he heard an *aww* or two coming from the direction of his female relatives. She pulled until he moved closer and their heads were brushing together. Her teeth grazed his earlobe and he had to bite the inside of his cheek to keep from moaning. He was sure from a safe distance this looked like a couple's embrace, but he could feel the menace coming off in waves from the woman in his arms, and still his cock throbbed from the closeness.

"This is all your fault, Gael Montez," she hissed. "We have to come clean. We can't keep pretending until I leave tomorrow." There was a little panic in her voice, but there was also a breathlessness there that he thought had more to do with how close they were standing than their conundrum.

He cursed the frisson of pure lust—yes, lust; he was done fooling himself that it was anything else—and gripped her hips, eliciting an extremely satisfying surprised gasp out of her. "I'm not the one who drove out here when there was a storm warning for the afternoon, Perla. And you can't take it back. A deal's a deal. You know we can't tell my mother we were lying."

"Get a room, you two!" Gabi, that instigator, yelled from the couch where she was playing with the dogs.

"Keys, sweetheart," he teased and this time her teeth did a lot more than graze his ear.

"So testy," he said, pulling away from her before she pulled a Mike Tyson.

"I'll go get your stuff." He winked at her as she sent him a dirty look, which made his dick impossibly harder. If he could, he'd put her over his shoulder and carry her to the nearest bedroom until he had her screaming his name.

"Did Brigida clean the cottage this morning, Gaelito? I don't want Perla staying over there if it's not clean." And he needed to get himself together; his mother and grandmother were in the room.

"Cottage?" Perla asked cautiously, and Gael almost grinned as he heard his sister's explanation.

"Yeah, you two will have your own little love nest."

Nightmare. She was in a nightmare. And the kicker was that if this wasn't a hellscape of her own making, this would've been the stuff of her wildest fantasies. Snowed in with the man she'd been in love with for as long as she could remember, in a picturesque little beach cottage while his family—whom she adored—made cooing noises at what a cute couple they made.

Yeah, it would've been her literal dream if it wasn't a real-life horror show. And the snow was still falling in heavy sheets, covering the entire property in fluffy white powder. She was looking out the window at the "cottage" she'd be staying in, which was just a few yards away from the main house. After Perla recovered from the initial shock of being stranded with Gael and his family, Gabi explained the cottage was Gael's private space. Speaking of Gael—that coward—he'd run off somewhere as soon as she'd caved and agreed to stay until the snow passed. Probably to figure out how to torture her some more.

And damn it all, the cottage was darling. From where she stood, she could see the two picture windows on either side of the door and the small stone fireplace.

"It's pretty cozy in there. Are you sure you're up for it?" Perla jumped when she heard Gabi's friendly voice behind her, and even though she was strung as tightly as she'd ever been, hearing her old friend did help her frazzled nerves.

"This is a really bad idea, Gabi," Perla whispered, looking around the kitchen like a caged animal, expecting Abuela or Veronica to find them and uncover the lie.

"Well, no. It's not a good idea at all." Perla's stomach flipped at Gabi's typically unfiltered honesty. "But it's too late to take it back now. Mami had a really rough couple of years, Perla. Like really bad." Gabi's voice broke on the last few words, and now that Perla was looking closely, she could see the drawn expression on her face. Veronica's health crisis had taken its toll on the whole family. "She's so happy to have you here. Last year we spent the holidays with her in the ICU."

Perla's heart lurched as she saw the pain on her old friend's face. Veronica's health was not Perla's responsibility, that was true, but she couldn't bring herself to resent Gabi or Gael for trying to keep their mom happy. She didn't have a mother who meant the world to her, who had protected her or whom she felt protective toward. But she knew that was what Veronica was to her children, and no matter how annoyed she was at Gael, she would not mess up the Montez's Nochebuena.

"All right," she said without anger. "But you need to talk to your brother. There will be no funny business. I get my own bed."

Gabi's face paled slightly at the mention of the bed. "Please tell me there's more than one bed, Gabriela."

"There's a pull-out couch," Gael's sister hedged. "The cottage's more like a suite than an apartment," Gabi explained, and Perla wanted to scream. But before she could list her many concerns with the plan,

Veronica and Gael walked in. At least he had the decency of looking somewhat worried.

"Okay, querida. I took a quick look at the cottage—"

"You didn't have to do that. It must be freezing out there and slippery," Perla said with concern, but Veronica waved her off with a smile.

"Gaelito built a covered walkway from the main house to it. Always so smart," she told her son, pushing up to kiss him on the cheek. "You've got fresh blankets and towels in there and I brought some almond creamer. I know you can't do regular milk in coffee." If she'd had any doubts about staying they were laid to rest in that instant. Veronica was positively beaming at the prospect of having Perla stay with them. She couldn't be selfish, not on this. "If I would've been informed about my son's new relationship status…" She offered a wink to soften the admonishment. "I would've made sure I had all the things you like, Perlita, but someone was keeping his secrets extremely under wraps as usual."

Despite Veronica's attempt to chastise them, Perla felt her throat tighten with emotion at her words. How did she remember? Perla had not had a cup of coffee with these people in at least six years, and still they knew how she liked it. Her own mother would probably be hard-pressed to list even two of her favorite foods, let alone details like what kind of creamer she liked.

"That's so kind of you. Thank you. And this relationship status change is very recent."

"Like super *super* recent, veritable breaking news," drolled Gabi, making Perla's face heat.

"Of course, mija. And don't be embarrassed about staying with Gael. We're a modern family," Veronica assured Perla, with a peck on the cheek. "Gabi's girlfriend stayed with us for Thanksgiving and we were so happy to have her here. I just want my kids and their partners at home with us."

The word *partner* landed like a punch to the gut. She looked up at Gael and saw that he wasn't faring much better. This white lie was turning into something perilous, and Perla was very aware that the biggest casualty would be her heart.

"Vamos, let me get you settled in," Gael said as he tugged on her hand. She should pull away. She should be furious with him, but he was looking at her with concern and with a tenderness she craved more than she would like to admit. She let him lead her to the mudroom, where she donned her coat and slipped her feet into too-big rain boots. They stepped out to find the wind howling all around them. The covered path protected them, but not completely, and it was freezing. The drive to the airport would've been terrifying in this. Even a thirty-second walk felt like a battle against the elements. But Gael's big body was right behind her as they made their way up the path, and no matter how things had been with them recently, she knew in her heart that if she stumbled he would catch her.

"Welcome to my casita," he announced without a hint of irony in his voice as they reached the red door with a circular window that let her see into the place she'd be spending the night.

They left their boots outside and stepped into the small cottage. The fire was roaring, making the space warm and toasty. The furniture was all designer. Lots of dark wood and soft, supple leather. Still, it looked inviting, like everything in Gael's home did. Except here there were not colorful cushions or knickknacks on the mantel. This place was more subdued, more masculine.

This was Gael's private space.

It was an open floor plan, just like the house. A small kitchen to the side, with stainless steel appliances and glass-front cabinets. A small table for two was set, there was an armchair with a reading lamp by the fireplace, and right beyond it he'd installed a floor-to-ceiling bookshelf. That was when she noticed the two paintings above his fireplace, and butterflies started flying in circles in her belly.

"You got the Jorge Meriño pieces," she said in surprise.

"I did." He was so nonchalant about it, as if it was no big deal for him to have two paintings by her favorite artist prominently displayed here. To be fair, Gael liked Meriño, too. He also knew the artist was her absolute favorite. This had been another thing they'd had in common, after all.

Perla always loved art; one of the few good things she'd gotten from her mother was her eye for it. When she and Gael started seeing each other, she'd discovered that he was also an art lover. They'd loved to go down to the city for shows and art gallery openings, especially ones displaying up-and-coming Latinx artists.

Their shared passion for art was something she hadn't thought about in years. Unlike the books and movies there was a difference in access to art for them that made it less real somehow. Back then Perla arrived to the shows like a collector, ready to buy a piece if she liked something. Meanwhile, Gael had only been an admirer, and on the occasions she offered to buy him something as a gift, he'd turned her down. But now he was a movie star, a man who could have anything and anyone he wanted.

Seeing one more thing they'd shared just made the fact that he wasn't truly hers, that he'd never be hers, again more painful. She held her breath and let it out slowly as she took in the pieces. She loved Meriño's aesthetic. He painted beautiful women with skin the color of graphite dressed in flowing gowns. They always wore white and had bright red hibiscus flowers in their hair. One of Perla's most prized possessions was one of his paintings. "When did you get these?" she asked, a little breathless, trying and failing not to read too much into this.

"The Luna Gallery in Tribeca. They just had a show of contemporary Ethiopian artists—I got a painting for my place in LA. I've bought a few pieces from them over the years."

That Ethiopian artist exhibit had been for VIPs only. She hadn't been able to go, but heard that the pieces all sold within a few hours. That meant Gael had been there on opening night. She'd taken him to Luna years ago when they were dating. But she had no idea he'd continued to go there on his own. This was…she didn't know what it was.

He was looking at her with that coy expression she remembered. It usually meant he knew he was about to get called out on something and was thoroughly prepared with a smart-ass comment. And Perla *had* questions. Why did he have these paintings in particular? Why did he keep going to the gallery she'd taken him to so long ago? What did this all mean? But as much as she wanted to ask, the truth was, none of it was any of her business anymore.

Gael Montez was not her business.

She returned her gaze to the two paintings and admired them for a moment, before offering him the sincerest smile she could muster. She needed some distance from Gael before she said something that would make the next twenty-four hours a lot more awkward than necessary. "They look really nice. I think I'm going to go back to the house," she said with a casual shrug she was not feeling. "I told your mom I'd come back to play dominoes with her, Gabi and Abuela. I also have to call Esmeralda."

She expected him to feign indifference, to let her walk out like he didn't care what she did. Instead, he answered the questions she hadn't asked out loud. "I got them because they reminded me of you." There was a tightness to his voice that she wanted very much not to read into. She had to get away from him before she said something she could not take back.

She stopped right by the door, reeling from the emotions she'd felt in the past couple of hours. She should probably confront him. Remind him it had been because of his choices that he'd lost her. Tell him how much it hurt her when he cast her aside. But she wouldn't give him any more of herself. Gael would never get any more of her tears. She just walked to the door instead. Before she walked out, she looked at him over her shoulder and said, "I never took you for the sentimental type."

She didn't feel an ounce of satisfaction in finally getting the last word.

Seven

"I can't believe the planes are grounded for the next day and a half," Perla lamented, tossing her cell phone aside after her call with the crew. She picked up the domino she'd been about to use for a play and tapped it on the table. She looked worried, upset. And he wished it didn't hurt to know that it was because she didn't want to be around him.

"You can stay with us as long as necessary, mi amor," his mother said sincerely. "It's been a delight to have you here." Veronica's comforting words only seemed to sink Perla into a deeper misery.

"I can't impose on all of you like that," Perla protested as his mother, sister and grandmother plied her with words of encouragement.

They'd made a mess of this.

Scratch that. *He'd* made a mess of this.

Against his best judgment, he walked over and put an arm around her, and it was a testament to how upset she was that she didn't fight him. She just sighed and burrowed into him. She let the whole weight of her body rest against him and he held her up. She looked up at him for a second, the winged eyeliner a little smudged now at the end of an emotional and chaotic day. "It was going to be my first Christmas with Esme's family," she explained, and she didn't have to say why that meant a lot to her. He knew how things had been with her mother. She was going to finally spend the holidays with family who treated her like they wanted her there. And now she would miss it. Right then Gael decided he would do whatever it took to give her a good Christmas. In a couple of days she would drive out of his life for good, but he'd give her two perfect days.

He lifted her chin so that she looked at him. "You're with family here, Perla. We'll take care of you." She didn't look convinced in the slightest, but she had too much home training to scoff in front of his mother and grandmother.

The girl he'd known and loved—yes, loved—had turned into a woman who was still searching for home. Perla may have found her confidence, but in some ways she was still lost, still looking for the unconditional love she'd never had, and he would make it his mission to ensure she got as much warmth and family as she could take in the next forty-eight hours. And because his family was the most extra in the world, soon they had Abuela, Gabi, Veronica and even the dogs coming in for a group hug.

"Mija, I know you're disappointed that you won't be with your sister in Punta Cana, but we will make sure you have a great Nochebuena with us," Veronica assured Perla as she pressed a kiss to her head.

"That's right, and I already have a few jobs for you, especially setting the table and getting everything pretty for our dinner. I was going to have Gaelito do them, but we know that boy has no finesse." Everyone laughed at Abuela's teasing, and Perla gave them all a watery smile.

"Thank you. I feel terrible about crashing your holiday plans like this—"

"Crashing?" his mother cried in horror at the suggestion Perla was not implicitly a part of every Montez family holiday. "You're family, baby. Gaelito's girlfriend." Gael felt her stiffen in his arms at the mention of their "relationship," but Perla was back on full fake-it-till-you-make-it mode, and just nodded.

"Thank you," she said, again, and when she looked up at Gael with those big stormy eyes, watery from unshed tears, something inside him cracked wide open.

"You're exactly where you belong," he told her, and to his surprise he felt the truth of those words in his very soul. He'd make sure he delivered on his promise to her.

"What are you doing?" Perla jumped at least a foot in the air when she heard Gael's voice, and then almost passed out when she turned to answer him and ended up face-to-face with a naked and very muscular tanned torso.

"Aren't you cold?" she asked irritably, instead of answering his question. Not that she could even put thoughts together when her brain kept trying to make her count the abs on his stomach.

Was that an eight-pack?

In college he'd had a swimmer's body, tight and lean, but not much bulk. He was so tall, it wasn't as if he needed the muscles to garner attention, but she guessed in Hollywood the more the better, at least when it came to brawn.

"I'm not," he said, running a hand over his chest as a self-satisfied smile tugged up his stupid, gorgeous mouth. "I asked you a question, Perla."

She furrowed her brow, trying extremely hard to recall what she could've possibly been doing before Gael short-circuited her brain with his abdominal muscles and extremely smooth, deeply bronzed skin.

"Um, what was I doing?" She looked down at her hands and finally her brain came back online. "I was decorating your tree." She'd found the little fake fir hidden in a corner next to a box full of ornaments and lights. "I wanted to make the place a bit more festive since all the Christmas spirit seems to be relegated to the main house." Apparently she said the wrong thing because now he was the one looking all flustered.

"Aren't *you* cold?" he asked—or growled if one was to get specific—pointing at her legs. She'd changed into something more comfortable while he was in the shower, and it seemed he'd noticed. He ran his gaze over her pajamas a few times, and she did not miss that he kept stalling on the spot where her shorts ended and her butt began. His eyes left a trail of heat all over her skin, enough to make her shiver. And yeah, they were *pretty short* shorts. In her defense, she had packed for a trip to the tropics.

"I am, a little, but this is the only kind of pj's I have, and as much as I love those faux leather leggings, they're not very comfortable to sleep in."

Okay, the hard staring was getting a little awkward.

And now he was walking away and going to the bedroom. God, had he always been this rude? With his family he'd been more or less normal, but since they'd come back to the cottage he'd been broody and short with her. And okay, she hadn't exactly been warm either, but this situation was nerve-racking.

"Here." His sharp voice resounded in the small space, and Perla looked up to find Gael holding up what looked like a pair of joggers.

She narrowed her eyes at him without making a move to take the pants. "Gael, you're almost a full foot taller than me. Those won't fit me. Also, I'm a bit curvier in certain areas." He directed his gaze at the area she was referring to, lips wrapped around his teeth, before facing her again.

"You can cuff them."

Was he giving her orders?

She crossed her arms over her chest, suddenly feeling contrary. "*No.* If you have a problem with what I'm wearing, I suggest you stop looking." With that she turned around and made sure her bottom was on full display as she bent down to pick up the box of ornaments she'd found. He could sound as mad as he wanted, but she'd seen him checking her out. She'd gained a bit of weight in the past few years, but for the first time in her life she felt comfortable in her own skin. Her mother had always drilled into her that she didn't have "the height for curves" and she'd always obsessed about dieting and her weight, but like most of the things her mother advised her on, Perla realized it hadn't been good for her.

So yeah, her butt was a bit bigger and her curves more generous, and she loved her body this way. And from the groaning and teeth-sucking behind her she assumed Gael didn't hate it, either. But for the sake of her own sanity, she ignored him and focused on wrapping fairy lights around the tiny tree.

"I don't want a tree in here," he finally said, his voice tight. He was such a grump about everything. He'd never been much for holiday cheer, but this year he was a full-on grinch. She turned around and found him looking at her with that terse expression, like having her in his space made his skin crawl.

"What's your problem, Gael? There are trees next door and you don't glare at them like you want to murder them. You used to be fine with decorating." She remembered driving over from her family's sumptuously decorated mansion in Greenwich to his house one year and going to Target with Gael to buy a new tree and outdoor decorations. It had been after he'd gotten paid for one of his first commercials. He picked out every ornament with such care. Perla had noticed some of them had been hanging on the new tree in his mother's living room. But as cheerful as things were in the main house, Gael's little space was...stark.

"I've had a hard time getting into the Christmas spirit in the past few years," he muttered and wouldn't even look at her as he talked. When they'd been together he'd confessed to her that his father had left their family during the holidays, and she wondered if that was what all this was about. Or if it had to do with...nope, not going there.

"Why are you being like this, Gael?" she asked, and his nostrils flared, his big hands twitching at his sides. She felt diminutive in front of him. His massive body towering over her. Gael had always been beautiful, but now he was Hollywood handsome. Almost too perfect. Skin polished, bright white veneers in his mouth, everything about him groomed to the maximum. Even in joggers and a sweatshirt there was something about him that made her want to stare. And that should intimidate her, because aware as she was of his perfection, she knew she was far from it. She was pretty; she knew that. And she appreciated her looks and knew what complemented her attributes. But she wasn't movie-star beautiful and that was what Gael was around every day. People whose job description included achieving almost unnatural levels of physical exquisiteness.

And yet, there was no denying the heat in his

eyes as he looked at her. It was almost menacing in its intensity, but she knew now, like she always had, that she would always be safe with Gael Montez. Well, at least her body would be—her heart was another story.

"I don't want to talk about any of that, and I'm sure you don't want to hear it," he said, reminding her that she'd posed a question.

"Sure, why don't you tell me how to feel, Gael? That's always been a special skill of yours." She knew that was not the way they would arrive at civility, but she was tired of his sulking.

She could see his jaw working, and a flush of pink working up his throat. She should leave this alone. This could not lead anywhere good. She'd already felt what his touch did to her. Already confirmed that the years and the distance had done nothing to temper her feelings for him, and here she was provoking him. Goading an answer out of him that would wreck her no matter what it was. And he *would* tell her, because Gael had never been a coward. And he'd already called her bluff once today.

He moved fast and soon she was pressed to a wall or a door, she didn't really care, because all of her concentration was going toward Gael's hands on her. His massive, rock-hard body pressed to her, and she wished, really wished, she had the strength to resist him. But all she did was hold on tighter when he pressed his hot mouth to her ear.

"I've told myself a thousand times today that I'm not supposed to want you as much as I do." He sounded furious and if she hadn't known him as well as she did she would've missed the regret lacing his words. He gripped her to him, and desire shot up inside her like Fourth of July fireworks, from her toes and exploding inside her chest.

"Wouldn't it be something if we could make ourselves want the things that we can actually have?" she said bitterly. He scoffed at that, and she didn't know if it was in agreement or denial of what she'd said. It was impossible to focus with his hands sliding over her like they were. She had never been able to put up much resistance when Gael had his focus on her. After a moment he pulled back. His eyes were bleak as he looked at her, and she dearly wished knowing he hadn't walked away unscathed didn't matter as much as it did.

"I don't want to talk about it." It. I-T. She had no idea what the *it* even was. It could've been so many things. His father's abandonment, their relationship and how it had been laid to waste. The years they'd had and lost, everything they could never get back. Two letters to encompass so much loss and heartbreak. There were things to say, so many. But she could not make herself say a word. The pain in his eyes wouldn't let her.

He ran a hand over his head, like he didn't know where to start. Like this was all too much for him, and for a moment she thought he would actually walk away, leave her standing there.

He kissed her instead.

Eight

<u>H</u>e'd almost told her everything. About what his father had said the night he walked out on Gael, his mom and sister. Almost confessed the real reason why he broke it off with her six years ago. Truth was like an avalanche roiling in him. But that was his baggage to carry, not hers. He could not change what was, the way he'd hurt her or the fate of the men in his family. But he could make these days good for her. He could get all the way out of his feelings and focus on Perla. He *could* take charge and give them both a much-needed release. The feel of her lips on him had dogged him all day. And now here she was, perfect and soft in his arms. Kissing him with a hunger that set his blood on fire. He tried to

think of something in the past six years that had felt this real, and he could not come up with a single one.

"I can't stop thinking about your mouth," he said, almost grudgingly, as she grazed his neck with her teeth.

"Well, if it makes you feel any better it's definitely mutual," she answered with a sexy little growl as she hooked her legs around him.

He'd told himself so many times after the breakup that she deserved better. Someone who could love her like she needed. Someone who could protect her heart. Told himself again and again that person couldn't be him. That no matter how much he tried, he was destined to break her heart. That his feelings for her had just been fleeting, a passing infatuation. But his reaction to her now, the frantic hunger he felt for her, told a very different story.

"Can I?" he asked as he rubbed his thumb over a hard nipple. He was eager to see her reactions; he'd always loved how expressive she was. How she didn't know how to hide her desire. She always showed him everything he made her feel. It had been like an addiction when they'd been together. He would spend hours exploring her. His hands on her skin, and his eyes pinned to her face, marveling at the way she'd squeeze her eyes shut, or let her mouth fall open from pleasure.

"Mmm," she moaned as he circled one taut tip with his thumb. And his mouth watered with the need to taste all the places he hadn't touched in so long. Perla had been…inexperienced in college. Gael had been her first everything. And even if he'd never admitted it, he'd fucking loved being the first man to ever see her fall apart in his arms.

"You like it when I touch you like this?" he asked, before dipping his head to mouth a nipple over her shirt.

"You know I do." He smiled at how put off she sounded, but her gray eyes, which had been so cold only a minute ago, were glowing. Gael wanted to see her burning for him.

He liked his sex dirty. And this woman right here, she had his head full of all kinds of filthy things. And right below that urge, there was a much more dangerous impulse, but he smothered that thought before it could get any oxygen. He brought his focus back to Perla. To the way she felt under his hands, perfect.

Still, she looked a bit shy as she took his hand, guiding it under her T-shirt. It was a black, longsleeved tee that had the words Gracefully Furious in pink font. He had to bite back a smile, because that was exactly how he would describe her. He'd always been drawn to her wit and that palpable fragility in her, but now there was a boldness there, too, and that made her irresistible.

Every thought other than touching her flew out of his head when he palmed the warm, soft skin under her shirt. She didn't say a word as he ran the heel of his hand up her ribs and then to the slope of her breast. They were small and pert, and they were...bare.

"No bra? That's different," he said, voice dripping with want as he worried a nipple between his thumb and index finger, making her mouth open in a silent moan.

"I don't like them. I never did. And now I only wear them if I have to," she told him, her back arching as she pushed herself into his hand.

"That is a dangerous piece of information to have. How will I get through the next day knowing the only thing between my hand and these beauties is one layer of clothes?" He leaned in to kiss her, a quick glide of his tongue with hers, and she opened up for him hungrily. Her mouth hot on his as he took small nips of her bottom lip. God, he could devour her. "I'm going to put my mouth on them now."

"Please." The little sounds she made were driving him absolutely crazy. This woman begging for him was almost overwhelming. He applied himself to touching her, ran the pads of his thumbs over each of her nipples, tracing with his fingers the places he'd taste.

"There's a rosy pink right under the brown of your skin, and when you're like this it flushes. I want to see the other places where you're a little pink, baby." And there was no stopping his mouth.

"Oh, my God," Perla moaned as she writhed in his hands. He bent his head and circled the hard tip of his tongue around the peaks of her breasts and when he flicked them with his finger…that got him another delicious sound of pleasure. With every touch, she pressed herself closer to him and now her legs were wrapped around him, so tightly that he could feel her heat through those sinful little shorts, and he was sure she could feel the base of his painfully hard cock.

"You feel that, sweetheart?" he asked as he nipped on one of her earlobes. "You feel how hard I am for you?" He thrust against her, and she rocked to meet him. He was careening into a series of extremely bad decisions, he knew that, and still his hands roamed down to the soft skin of her belly.

"Are you ready for me?" he asked as his hand snaked down to her core.

"So ready," she gasped when his fingers grazed against the curls covering her folds.

"You're aching for this, aren't you? When was the last time someone touched you like this?" He had no idea why he was going there. If he was smart he'd leave that door firmly shut, but something in him needed to hear that no one made her feel like he did.

"Six years to be exact," she said in a breathy whisper as she reached for his hard cock. Her grip was like a vise and he could not think. He plunged into her hand viciously, even as he tried to process what he'd just said.

"Mmm," he grunted, dizzy from pleasure. "Six years?" he asked, fuzzy thoughts starting to become clearer. Six years; she hadn't been with anyone in six years? He'd broken her heart so badly that she hadn't been with anyone else?

And now he was doing this with her when he knew there was no possible future for them.

Fuck. He needed to stop this. *Now*.

"What?" she asked breathlessly as he unwound

her legs from around his waist, jumping back like her skin was scalding him. She looked drunk from his kisses, so utterly edible. But he knew what the right thing to do was. He wouldn't go any further without being certain she would not regret this later. And today had been too much of a roller coaster for sex to be anything other than a terrible idea. But it seemed Perla was going to be pissed at him anyway.

"You're going to regret this later," he told her, rubbing his mouth with the back of a shaky hand.

She flinched like he'd slapped her. Her expression went from dreamy and warm, to shuttered and embarrassed. "You don't have the slightest clue about my regrets, Gael," she said stonily, "but you're right about one thing. This is a mistake." She was already pushing him back so she could get away.

"It's not a mistake. I just don't want to complicate things more than they already are." *Because I'm almost certain that I still have feelings for you, and doing this will probably end with you hating me even more than before.*

"It's not that I don't want you, Perla—"

"Oh, my God," she screamed, her face a mask of horrified embarrassment. "Please, Gael, spare me the 'it's not you, it's me' rerun from college." Perla was not even looking at him. Her hands crossed over her chest and her face miserable. She seemed seconds from starting to cry. "I haven't forgotten what you said." She held up a hand at him, her expression forbidding. "No need to tell me again. Let's just pretend none of this happened and try to get through tonight and tomorrow," she said miserably and stormed off to the bedroom. He could hear her moving around the room quietly as he stood there like a statue looking at the bare little tree with its twinkling lights. She never even got to put on the ornaments.

He was *such* an asshole. He knew that adding a fake relationship with Perla to the already shitty mix of feelings that usually cropped up for him around the holidays was a terrible idea, and less than twelve hours in, he already had her on the verge of tears. His father had been right; the Montez men really could not stop themselves from hurting the women they cared about.

All those years ago, on another Christmas Eve when his life had fallen apart, his father had warned him of that fact. After disappearing for over a week, Gabriel Montez had shown up at dinnertime on Noche-buena smelling like booze and another woman's per-fume. His mother, finally done with years of putting up with her husband's philandering, had kicked him out.

Gael wasn't sure what it was about that particular time, after so many others, that seemed to take. But she'd stood firm in her best red dress with Gabi crying against her legs and demanded he leave them alone. Gael remembered that he expected his dad to do his usual round of begging. To fling excuses and endear-ments at his mother until she relented. To his surprise, without a word, his father had gone to the bedroom he'd shared with his wife for over fifteen years, packed a suitcase and after kissing him and his sister goodbye, walked out of their house for the last time.

Gabi and Veronica watched the man go with tears streaming down their faces, but Gael ran after him. Angry and confused, he demanded that his father explain why he was abandoning his family. Why he kept hurting his mother. Why he didn't love them. His father had lifted a shoulder and said, "The Montez men are no good to their women, mijo. No matter what we do, we end up destroying the women we love." He shook his head sadly, like he could not understand it himself. "It's a curse." With that, he bent down to kiss ten-year-old Gael on the forehead, got in his car and drove away.

Over the years Gael told himself a lot of things regarding what his father had said that night. That his dad had been weak and selfish, and trying to make excuses for his bad behavior. That he'd chosen to fail his family, that he cheated because he wanted to. That he would never be that kind of man. He'd spent eighteen years telling himself that he'd be different from his father, and here he was hurting this woman, again. And what was any of this for? To pretend for a few days and then leave them both done in again?

Manolo had been right about one thing; with Perla and him it had to be all or nothing. He could not pretend with her; he couldn't only have her halfway. And that was why staying away from her had been the right thing, the safe thing. No matter how much he wanted her, how deep his need ran for her, he would *hurt her*.

It didn't matter what he wanted or, in this case, who. He was a Montez and Montez men ended up alone.

* * *

Perla: SOS...SOS!

Perla was well aware that her texting was a bit on the dramatic side today, but desperate times, and all that. She'd kissed Gael *again*. She almost did more than that, and then he'd pushed her away. God, how many times would she set herself up to be humiliated like that?

She'd just hide in the bedroom and pretend she was asleep when he came in to bed. Or maybe he'd sleep on the couch. She wished the idea made her feel better, but the thought of him sleeping in discomfort because he was trying to avoid her only sank her mood further.

He must think she was desperate. And the worst part was that she would've let him have her right there. She'd been aching for it. It was like she was a completely different person when she was with Gael. Reckless and impulsive, ruled by her desires.

She needed someone to talk her off this cliff, which seemed to be crumbling under her feet almost by the minute. Perla fired another message off to Marquito, Rodrigo's brother—and her closest friend. He was supposed to fly to the DR for Christmas, too, but had pulled out at the last minute, saying he had too much work with the awards season starting in January. Marquito was a stylist to some of Hollywood's A+ list, so he was spending the holidays in LA on his own. And Perla had been so caught up in drama today that she hadn't even checked up on him.

Marcos: Girl, you're not still trying to get on a plane, are you? I thought you were grounded until the storm passes.

The details of her breakup with Gael Montez weren't exactly public knowledge. She wasn't sure how he'd done it, but he'd managed to keep any mention of how their relationship ended out of the news. But she and Marquito went way back. Since his relationship with her asshole brother, Onyx, had crashed and burned years ago. And in the past year since their siblings rekindled their own romance they'd grown closer than ever. Which meant he knew all the sordid details about her and the Hollywood heartthrob.

Perla: No, I'm still in New York. No one's flying out of here for a while. I'm snowed in at Gael Montez's house in the Hamptons.

The three dots indicating that Marquito was typing up a message appeared immediately.

Marcos: You're what?! OMG PERLA SAMBRANO! Can I call you?

Perla cringed at the idea of Gael hearing her gab about her thirst for him while he was in the other room.

Perla: I can't. I'm in Gael's private cottage…because we sort of told his mom we're dating again.

A string of gifs appeared, which Perla supposed were trying to convey Marquito was not computing.

Marquito: For the love of all that is holy please let me call you.

As she considered what to do she heard a door open and close in the cottage. And a moment later through the bedroom window she saw Gael's tall figure walking out on to the boardwalk leading to the ocean. He looked so sad and alone, and Perla once again wondered what the hell she thought she was doing with this man. Sullenly, she tapped her screen and called Marquito. It didn't fully ring once before he picked up.

"I want the tea. All of it!"

Despite herself, Perla smiled at her friend's nosiness. "You're a chismoso," she told him, unable to mask the genuine affection in her voice.

"I do love my gossip, but come on, friend. *This is major.* What's going on? How did you end up in the Hamptons?"

She sighed before launching into a detailed explanation of the day's occurrences and almost couldn't believe herself that all that had happened in less than twelve hours.

"So you're spending Nochebuena with him and his family, pretending to be his girlfriend?" Marquito recapped.

"Correct."

"And you've already made out twice and are sleeping in the same bed tonight?"

Perla growled at Marquito's giddiness. "This is such a fun game. I'm so glad I called you."

"Perlita, babe, are you having just pants feelings for this boy or is your heart in the mix, too?"

And that was the question, wasn't it? One that she would be smart to answer sooner rather than later.

Still looking where she'd seen Gael's tall figure long after he disappeared from view, Perla sighed. "Maybe…" Lies. "Okay, not maybe, I do." She slumped on the bed feeling wrung out from the admission. It was one thing to barely acknowledge it to herself, but a whole other to say it out loud.

"Oh, friend." Marquito's gentleness as he spoke to her stung. She hated feeling pitiful and foolish.

"You know what's even more absurd?" Perla asked into the silence of the room as she shifted to get under the covers.

"What?" Marquito asked cautiously.

"I'd convinced myself that I was over him. It's barely been twelve hours, Marcos, and I can't breathe right if he's around. I can't *think* when I'm close to him." Perla squeezed her eyes shut as she thought of the way he'd touched her just minutes ago. The way his big hands had felt on her skin. "I've let him kiss me twice, and I know I'll do it again if he asks me."

"Oh, boy…Perla Marina Sambrano, you in danger, girl."

"I know," she said, resigned, and considered her options. This thing with Gael would end poorly. He was not interested in a relationship. As far as she could tell he hadn't had a serious girlfriend since they split up. It was probably unhealthy of her, but over the years she'd kept up with him, or at least with what the tabloids had to say, and he had not had a long-term relationship. He'd casually dated a model or a costar, but they never lasted.

Not that she was one to talk. She couldn't remember the last time she'd gone past a first date. But she had a lot going on; she didn't have the bandwidth for a relationship. She was just starting this new chapter in the family business. She was finally on her own and free from her mother's clutches for the first time in her life. She'd told herself she would focus on her career, that she'd take this time to figure out what she wanted. In conclusion, she should not want Gael Montez, but she still did.

"Perlita, are you still there?" Marquito's raspy voice yanked her out of her thoughts.

"I'm going to see where things go."

Perla thought Marquito's long exhale would be a preface to him trying to talk her out of it, but when he spoke, he surprised her. "Who am I to lecture you, babe? I keep falling headfirst into someone that I know isn't good for me. But I love him." Perla's heart ached for her friend, and she wished her brother wasn't such a selfish jerk.

"I'm sorry," she said sincerely. "I wish Onyx would get his head out of his ass."

"Nope, we're not touching my drama tonight. Perla. If you want that man, let yourself have him."

"I think I might," she assured her friend before ending the call. Anticipation roared under Perla's skin like the flames of a fire as she lay in Gael's bed. This was not a smart plan, but maybe that was why it needed to happen, because from how they'd both been thirsting after each other all day she knew all of this tension would need to be popped somehow. And wasn't it better to do it now? To stop fighting the inevitable and slake this lust that was clouding her judgment? No one had ever done to her what Gael could. He made her feel like a goddess when he looked at her with lust burning in his eyes. It was impossible not to want to snatch some of that when it was within her grasp.

She'd known that was the reason why she'd barely even kissed another man in all these years. It was like having to live on fast food when you'd gotten used to filet mignon. And she wanted another taste of him, even if was just one last goodbye. She'd wait for him to get back, and she'd fill Gael Montez in on why the only way for them to fake this relationship convincingly was to burn off some of this sexual tension. She had a few suggestions on how exactly they could do that.

Nine

"Damn, bro. I can feel the waves of tension coming off you all the way from here."

"Can't I have ten seconds to myself in this place?" Gael made a frustrated noise with his back to his sister. He'd come here after Manolo had called him for the fourth time in an hour to talk about the project he was insisting Gael take, even after he'd told him on the plane he wasn't interested. Manolo, as always, had not been happy that Gael didn't take his advice, but his uncle had gone into a full rage when Gael told him he'd accepted the role for the Rios series. The man had launched into a tirade about how he was throwing away the work they'd done to build his brand. Gael hadn't been in a mood to be handled and had ended the call. Hell, he wasn't in the mood for anything. Not after how things had gone with Perla.

He was leaning on the rails on the small pier he'd built on the property. There were lamps overhead lighting the path, but Gael had chosen a dark corner to come and think. He was still at a loss of what to do about the woman he'd left in his house looking miserable.

"So testy," Gabi responded without heat, and walked over to him until they were standing side by side. She didn't say anything, just kept watch with him in silence until he was ready to talk.

"We should've gone to the condo in Ponce," he told her.

Gabi scoffed and wrapped an arm around his waist. "You know Mami can't handle Christmas in Puerto Rico yet. She'll want to go visit everybody, and there'll be people coming through the house all day. She's not well enough for all that. Besides, she loves it here. This is her favorite place." His sister tightened her hold on him and he was grateful for her anchoring presence in this moment when he felt so close to drifting away.

His mother did love the ocean. When he was a kid, she'd talk about her own childhood in Puerto Rico. Of growing up in Ponce and walking to the beach for a swim every morning, and he'd dreamed of giving her that. Of buying a little corner of ocean for her. And now he'd done more than that. His mother had an oceanfront condo in her beloved Ponce, a house in the Los Angeles hills with stunning views of the Pacific Ocean, and a mansion in the Hamptons with a private beach. He dearly wished he could feel something other than exhaustion when he thought about all of it.

"I've made a mess of things with Perla," he blurted out. "Again."

His sister let out a long, sympathetic sigh, and he could feel her head shaking against his shoulder. "You two are hopeless. I thought Perla would be smarter than you, but it seems like you have very adverse effects on each other's intelligence. Dummies." Gabi's sad laugh blended with the crashing waves of the ocean. It was too dark to see her, but he could picture the sardonic smile on her lips. "You kissed her again, didn't you?"

"Yes." Gael put his head in his gloved hands as he waited for his sister to ream him out. Whatever she was about to tell him, he deserved it. Because he knew better. The kindest thing a Montez man could do for a woman he cared about was to leave her alone. What he ought to do right now was walk into the house and come clean to his mother, then stay as far from his ex as he could.

But the need to be around her was like a sickness. "I thought I was past this."

"Past lusting after the woman you've been in love with since sophomore year of college?"

"I'm not in love with Perla," he argued weakly. "I *can't* be in love with her. I can't be in love with anyone—*you know why.*"

This time his sister's sigh was the opposite of

sympathetic. "Gael, please, you have to stop with this 'I'm cursed' nonsense. Our father was a no-good bum, and he should've never—"

"It's true, though." Gael turned to his sister, grateful for the semidarkness, hoping it hid some of the agony on his face.

The blue tint of the moonlight cast his sister in a gloomy light, and he wondered how much her somber expression mirrored his. "I wish I'd told Mami about that bullshit you've had in your head all this time."

"You can't," Gael warned.

"I won't," she sighed, tiredly. "If I haven't done it in all this time, I'm not going to do it when she's so frail. It would kill her to know you've been doing this to yourself."

"I'm not doing anything to myself," he answered stubbornly. "I should've been more careful, but as soon as I saw her it was like all the lectures I'd been giving myself burned to ashes. I've fronted like this was all for Mami. But that's bullshit. I wanted her. It's like my self-control evaporates whenever Perla's near. And all I do is hurt her."

"God, you're such an idiot." As far as confidantes went, his sister was not a coddler, but at least she was honest.

"You hurt her because you keep hanging on to that stupid curse idea and listening to Manolo. There's no curse, Gael. You broke up with her in college because you let Manolo convince you that your career was going to suffer if you had a girlfriend. And you're hurting her now because you're choosing to believe our father's ridiculous excuse to justify his cheating. The man could not take responsibility for anything."

"If none of it is true, how come I left Perla crying in the cottage? I've barely been around her for a day and I've already made her miserable."

"Why is she crying?" His sister's tone told him she already knew the answer.

"Because I told her she'd regret it if things went further."

Gabi made a sound that was a cross between sympathy and frustration. "You know, it's a good thing you figured out a way to channel this melodramatic streak of yours into an exorbitantly lucrative career, because you are too much sometimes."

"Way to kick a guy when he's down, sis."

"I'm not kicking you while you're down. I'm telling you to get over yourself. I don't know what you two were up to in that cottage, but by the way you were eyeing each other all day, I assume it had something to do with you and your very poorly concealed thirst." She held her hand up, as if she could sense he was about to protest. "Nope, I'm talking. You keep hurting Perla because you refuse to accept your feelings for her, and you're stubborn as hell. If it wasn't because this role came up, you would've spent the rest of your life wondering where you went wrong. What is so bad about you wanting Perla and her wanting you back?"

"Because it can't work." Gael wondered who exactly he was trying to convince.

"It certainly won't with that attitude," Gabi retorted, and she sounded like she was about to completely lose her patience. "Have you ever considered that if you just go with it, things may not seem so monumental? You're both young, hot and with money to burn. If you want something or someone, all you have to do is reach for it...or her."

"I don't know, sis." Gael considered his sister's words. Being around Perla today he felt like he had ants under his skin. Unsettled and frantic from wanting her. But maybe that was what he had to do. Just let this thing between them happen. Just let them run their course and then she would leave and his life would go back to normal. They were both adults, after all. If they went in with their eyes open, then they could walk away once it was over.

"You know what, Gabi?" he asked, a plan hatching in his head already. "I think you're right. I think I just need to go with it."

"What are you up to, Gael Alberto Montez?" Gabi asked suspiciously as they turned and headed back up the pier.

"You should be happy. I'm finally taking your advice," he said distractedly, his mind already picturing how he'd find Perla. Maybe she was already in bed.

"That's what I'm worried about."

"Don't worry about me, little sister," he told her as he bent down to kiss her forehead. "I have it all under control."

The last thing he heard as he walked up the stone path to the cottage was his sister's laughter. "Famous last words."

* * *

Perla woke up on a slab of granite. Of very warm, very bronzed granite.

"Oh, Lord," she whispered as the events of the previous night, and day, came roaring back to her. She was in bed with Gael Montez, and despite it being a California King, she'd somehow ended up sprawled on top of him. He was significantly larger than she was, which meant that with her fully on top of him, she could still see a lot of golden brown skin. She opened one eye, and yes, there was a good amount of sculpted muscle and delicious collarbone to admire. Her lips, which at the moment were exactly in the valley between his pecs, itched to pucker up and press a kiss on that smooth skin.

God, she couldn't even count the number of times she'd yearned to wake up like this again. Of getting to look her fill, to touch as much as she wanted. And she wanted. She wanted *so much*. She'd fallen asleep waiting for him to return, so she didn't get a chance to propose her plan to him. But she would as soon as he woke up. She'd be a fool to waste this chance. Because if one thing was certain, it was that this lust was not going anywhere.

She sensed something stirring at the foot of the bed and stiffened, wondering if she'd been thinking so loud she'd woken up Gael, then she felt it, a very warm vibration by her feet.

She sat up startled, and Gael, with his eyes still closed, shifted, until something started moving up his body under the blankets.

"What the hell?"

"It's just Chavi," he explained and lifted a hairless sphynx cat from under the covers.

"Oh, my," Perla said as the cat rubbed its tiny bald head against Gael's wrists. She purred like a little motorboat. "I thought you didn't like cats."

"I don't," he assured her as he ran a hand over the animal's back. "But she likes me, and my mother insists I need 'some kind of company.' Which means I got Chavienda for my birthday this year."

She couldn't help the laugh that exploded out of her. "You named your cat nuisance?"

He grinned at her and then winked, and goodness, the man really was beautiful. He was sitting up now and she could see the notches of his hips and that trail of brown hair leading to his...

"My eyes are up here, Perla." Oh, that was his sex voice, and wow, it still had a very strong effect on her. "And her name's nuisance in *Puerto Rican slang.*" Gael's voice snapped her out of lusting for him, and she kind of melted when she saw how gentle he was with the cat. "It's very fitting given her family situation."

Perla could not help the grin that tugged at her mouth. "So far she's been extremely well behaved, so she's not much of a nuisance. This is kitty slander."

"That's because you haven't looked closely at my coffee table. She loves to file her claws on it," Gael harrumphed as he swiftly grabbed the cat, put her out of the room and closed the door. He flopped back into the bed and smiled up at her.

"How did you sleep?" He sounded tentative, but there was something in his voice this morning that had not been there last night. Like some of that distance he'd been putting between them had been bridged.

"Good," she quipped as she warmed under his attentive gaze.

"I'm glad." He shifted so that the sheets revealed more of his skin.

It was exceedingly difficult to focus on what he was saying when she had over six feet of Puerto Rican male in his prime two feet away.

His mouth had always been a particular fixation of hers. The bottom lip was fleshier, but both were perfectly shaped, the top one a shade darker than the rest of him, but the bottom one was this enticing pink, and God, she loved tugging on it with her teeth. Sucking on it until she made his breath hitch. Her gaze locked on that mobile mouth. The way it stretched when he smiled, and parted just a little when he was deep in thought.

She'd never stopped wanting him. She might never stop. She wished she could be bold and ask for what she desired, but she didn't want him to push her away. Gael sucked in a breath as she worried her thumb over his lip, and then moved to clamp a hand on her wrist.

"Te agarre," he said, and that was exactly how she felt. Caught. Caught looking, caught wanting something she shouldn't and craved anyway.

Her body flushed hot and cold and her stomach fluttered frantically at his touch. His gaze moved up until they were looking at each other. And she could see it there, that fire in his eyes, *that want*. Gael may not be able to love her. He might not want a future with her, but he desired her. That heat in his eyes could be nothing else. And if this was all he could give her…she would take it. He pulled on her arm until their mouths were inches away, and her heart felt like it would burst through her chest.

"Quiero besarte," Gael whispered against her lips.

"But morning breath," she hedged breathlessly.

He smiled against her mouth and moved in closer until their foreheads were pressed together. "It doesn't bother me, sweetheart." She was melting, her bones and muscles softening with every word and every touch.

"Okay." She could hear the tremor in her voice as he moved in closer and shifted them until she was on her back and he was covering her. He was so big. This lusty god was everything she could see and feel, a complete assault on her senses. He brought their mouths together and gave her an achingly sweet kiss. While the others had been rushed and ravenous, this one was sultry and sensuous. He licked at the seam of her mouth, his tongue warm as he explored her, gliding against her own. All the while his hands roamed her body; he caressed her thighs, her calves, palmed her belly. Like he wanted to map every part of her. She ached for him with bewildering urgency. It was like she'd forgotten how to feel in these past six years and Gael's hands and mouth had woken up all those dormant sensations.

She ached for him. A dull, throbbing need pulsing at the apex of her thighs.

"Please, Gael," she whispered against his mouth, arching her back to press even closer to him.

"Mmm," he moaned and moved them again until

she was astride his hips. She could feel his erection prodding against her backside, and a shiver of lust coursed through her body. She wanted that, too, him deep inside her. She rubbed herself against Gael, eliciting a tortured sound from him.

"Come here," he told her, already reaching for her, and the demand in his voice with just a hint of possessiveness ignited her blood. She had no idea what happened between last night and the morning to change Gael's mind, but she would not question it. He kissed her hungrily, one hand at the nape of her neck, while the other skated up her belly. "Can I touch you here?" he asked as the tips of his fingers brushed the underside of her breast.

"Please," she begged as she went in for another kiss. Their tongues languidly tangled together as he played with her breasts. He plucked on a nipple and then the other, making liquid heat pool in her core.

"Oh, God," she gasped as he brought his other hand under her shirt.

"You like this?" he asked, and she only nodded, too turned on to make words. The way he touched her, like he owned her—it made her dizzy with lust. She wanted to ask for more, to take his hand and press it to where she pulsed for him, and just as she was about to do it, the door of the cottage crashed open, sending them both scrambling.

Ten

"Are you okay?" Gael asked Perla as she rushed to put on the jogger pants he'd gotten her, which *were* way too long, but still distractingly hugged the curves of her ass and hips.

It was going to be very hard to keep his hands off her today. And he still had no idea what he was doing. He had to talk to her, tell her that he still could not give her what she wanted. That he would not take more chances with her heart when he knew he'd never be able to be the man she deserved. That they could do this until she left. But right now he had to deal with his sister, who was hollering like a lunatic outside the bedroom.

"Jesus," Gael exhaled as he slid on a Henley and hurried to open the door of the bedroom. "I'll go deal with her. Take your time," he said to Perla, who was now looking through her bag.

"All right, thanks," she said, looking up at him. Her cheeks were still flushed, and her lips looked a little swollen from his kisses. He wished to every deity he could just kick his sister out and go back to what he was doing. But there was no way that was happening. Not on Christmas Eve.

"Chill out, Gabriela! What the hell?" he grumbled, reluctantly closing the door behind Perla.

The moment he set foot in the living room his pest of a sister wolf-whistled as she gave him a very thorough once-over and a goofy grin appeared on her face. "Oh, I see how it is."

"You see nothing," he muttered and pointed at the three insulated tumblers on the table. "Is one of those for me?"

Gabi nodded as she stared at the closed bedroom door. "Yes, the blue one's yours. So what exactly was occurring before I arrived?"

Gael ignored his sister's nosiness and picked up the piece of paper next to the coffee. It was a to-do list in his mother's handwriting. He smiled as he got himself caffeinated. First on the list was "come over and have breakfast with your elders." "Mami's in a mood today."

Gabi smiled and grabbed her own cup. "She is. She wants you to make the chocoflan and tres leches. I'm in charge of the pernil and the playlist." She glanced at the door again and smiled wide. "Abuela's requested that your girlfriend be in charge of setting the table."

Gael raised an eyebrow at that. "I'll tell her when she gets out of the shower."

"I take it things are marching smoothly, then?" Gabi thought she was cute.

Gael only nodded and kept gulping down coffee.

"You're no fun," his sister groused.

"And you're a busybody. We'll be at the house in twenty and then I'll bring all the stuff for the dessert here. That way Mami and Abuela have the big kitchen to themselves."

They talked about the plans for the evening as they sipped coffee, and after a while Perla stepped out of the bedroom. She looked adorable in another oversize sweater, this one a forest green, with very skinny jeans. Her face was free of makeup and her short black hair was sticking up in every direction. He wanted to ravage her. His heart pounded and his skin prickled whenever he saw her. He could tell himself, his sister and even Perla whatever he wanted, but in that moment he gave up on telling himself lies about what he was feeling for this woman.

"Morning," Perla said shyly as Gabi handed her the third coffee tumbler.

"Good morning," Gabi said cheerfully, while Gael put his arm around Perla and brought his mouth down to hers for a kiss.

"You used my toothpaste," he muttered against her mouth, tasting cinnamon and clove.

"Yes, I forgot mine," she told him a little breathlessly as they pulled apart.

He was a little deprived of oxygen himself, and still this felt right. Even if it was only for today.

"Mami sent Gabi with a list of what she needs us to help with and she wants us at the house for breakfast. Are you okay with that?" he asked quietly as Gabi sat on the couch playing with the cat.

Perla didn't respond immediately, her gaze fixed on something behind them. "You finished it," she said, pointing at the other side of the room. When he turned, he saw the little Christmas tree that he'd decorated after he'd come back and found her asleep.

"Yeah," he confirmed as Perla walked over to it, getting his sister's attention.

"Acho, Gael. Did you actually put up the tree?"

Perla turned to look at him, obviously curious for what he'd tell his sister. "Perla wanted it up."

"I did. Thank you." His pretend girlfriend offered him a happy little smile, and the warmth of it blazed all the way to his bones.

"Oh." There was a whole lot more to that one syllable that his sister kept to herself, but he wasn't trying to encourage Gabi and her opinions. His head was enough of a mess as it was. He took the few steps to reach Perla and put his arms around her. He'd always been like this with her. Couldn't keep his hands to himself.

"All right, lovebirds, Mami texted. Food will be ready in fifteen minutes. Gael, go brush your teeth,"

Gabi said with a flutter of her hand. "Go now while I'm still here. I'll keep Perla company."

He didn't call his sister a cockblock as he walked into the bedroom, but he thought it. He still couldn't muster up a negative feeling as he stepped into the shower. All he could think was that for the first time in a long time, he was looking forward to Nochebuena.

Things were decidedly different this morning. Gael not only had been extra handsy, but he'd also been like that in front of his *sister*. Now they were stepping out to go have breakfast with his mother and he was holding Perla's hand as they walked, like it was the most natural thing in the world.

"Are you still doing your famous desserts?" Perla asked as they carefully walked the path to the house. Gabi had filled her in on the duties that had been assigned to Gael.

"You remember that?" Gael sounded surprised. If he only knew that she had every detail about him permanently on tap. That there was nothing he'd ever told her that she didn't remember.

"Of course I do. Chocoflan and tres leches are your specialties. Do you still make extras?" She smiled at a memory of them making desserts the year before everything fell apart. As they worked, Veronica had informed her that Gael was a neighborhood legend due to his skills making the two desserts. After getting a job at one of the Latin markets in town when he was in high school, Gael started making them for his family and made extras for the neighbors. Every year after that the list of people he gave them to grew, and by the time he was in college he made a couple of dozen desserts every year, which he distributed to people in the neighborhood and a local senior center.

"Kind of. Not like I used to," he answered, pulling her out of her own head. Gael must've noticed something in her expression because he put a finger under her chin and tipped her face up to him. "Is something wrong?"

"What are we doing, Gael?" The words were out of her mouth before she could stop herself. It wasn't like the question wasn't warranted. He pursed his mouth as he considered what to say and she wished he wasn't wearing his sunglasses so she could look into his eyes.

"Right now the only thing I know for sure is that while you're here, I want more of you." He shook his head and his long hair grazed against his chin. She almost smiled thinking that now she was the one with the shorn hair and his was long enough to braid. "Having you in my bed this morning felt good. And holding you when my sister was with us felt even better. I don't have any answers other than that. I can't offer anything beyond this day and tonight."

She should've prodded then and told him he was acting like she was only a warm body, a convenient distraction. But she realized that even if he was, she wanted him anyway. If he felt the same, then today she'd pretend that he really was hers. Tonight she'd ask him to make love to her just as she'd intended, and in the morning she'd get in her car and finally move on with her life. Finally say goodbye to Gael Montez.

"We have today, then," she said, and pushed up to kiss him.

Eleven

"Gael!" Gabi called from behind him and as soon as he turned, a wet, cold clump of snow hit him right in the face.

"Eat it, sucker!"

He didn't have the chance to ask if it was on purpose, because his pain in the ass of a sister was already running toward him with another snowball.

"Oh, no, you don't," he called, bending down to pile some snow in his hands. "Perla, get behind me. She's ruthless."

He heard a snicker and turned around to see Perla packing a ball of her own.

"Good. I'll need reinforcements," he said, affecting the voice of his character in the Space Squadron, a military general who could blast fireballs from his

hands. "Heads up," he bellowed as he avoided another face full of snow and pelted his sister on the
elbow.

Perla was small but fast, and soon she was also
chucking snowballs in Gabi's direction. "Perla Sambrano, *do not* throw snow at my head!" his twin sister shrieked. "You know I don't like getting my hair
wet." Gael grinned like a loon when he heard Perla's
apology and then saw a snowball hit Gabi right in
the solar plexus.

"Yes!" he crowed, throwing a fist in the air as he
ran for cover. "Get her, babe!" The word was out of
his mouth before he could stop himself. Perla's hand
froze and the snowball she was packing crumbled
on her palm as she looked at him. What the hell was
going on with him? Why did he have to keep testing the boundaries? He had just come to a place that
worked for both of them, and already he was trying
to push past it into something else. But his annoying
sister wasn't done throwing snow at him.

"You're really gonna get it now, Gabriela Montez!" he yelled as he brushed snow off the back of his
head, grateful the fight distracted Perla from what
he'd just said. As soon as he stood up, snow hit him
from all directions; he gave up trying to throw his
own and covered his face with his hands. "Et tu,
Perla?" he joked and heard both women cackle with
laughter.

"You've been defeated," Perla boasted as she
made her way to him. She looked so happy, her face
open. Beaming. It was a wonder how he'd fooled

himself as long as he had when it came to his feelings for her. She filled him up. Seeing her smile always nourished something in him no one else ever could. There was this constant yawning void in him that even his loving family couldn't fill. It gnawed at him constantly, but her presence had always eased it. He'd felt the difference when he'd met her in college. And since he'd given her up it had just grown bigger. Fame, fortune...none of it could make it better. But today, seeing this Perla, whom he thought was lost to him forever, laughing with glee as she tossed snow up in the air, made his cup run over. Fulfilled and overflowing.

"I've been betrayed by my comrade," he said dramatically as he pulled on her snow-crusted glove and brought her in for an embrace. "I'm wounded," he whispered as he pressed his lips to her cold cheek.

"I can kiss it better," she told him, turning her face to him. Gael's whole body pulsed with something very close to happiness.

"Ew, get a room, you two. Come on, Mami's waiting!" Gabi yelled at them as she headed up the path to the house, but they ignored her, completely caught up in each other.

"Poor baby." Perla's voice was raspy as she brushed kisses on the spot on his neck where the snowball had landed. The skin there tingled from the icy flakes, and probably from feeling her hands on him. He wanted to say she had already made it better. He almost told her that he could see in color for the first time in years. That he could feel the chill on his face and the snow beneath his feet more vividly than he had almost anything else in these past six years. But he didn't say any of it. He wouldn't make declarations to this woman whom he would later betray. He would not make promises that he knew he'd never be able to keep.

"Are you sure you don't want to come make the desserts with us?" Perla asked as she put the lid on the bin of ingredients Veronica had lined up for them.

"Nah, my brother is the pro at the sweet stuff. I'm going to work on the playlist and get the living room set up for dancing while the pernil's in the oven. It'll just be us, but some of our neighbors may come by after dinner."

Gabi gave Perla one of those assessing looks she remembered from when they lived together in a college dorm. "Seems like you guys have figured out a way to make things work," she said, and if Perla didn't know her as well as she did, she wouldn't have heard the underlying question there. *Are you two really going to be able to keep it casual?*

Perla had no clue, and it seemed Gael wasn't faring any better. She'd practically swooned when he'd called her *babe*.

"Gael said he still makes the flans for the neighbors," she told Gabi in an attempt to deviate the conversation from feelings. "I can't believe he still does that."

Gabi furrowed her brow as if she wasn't certain what Perla was talking about, then realization washed over her face.

"He told you he only gives them to the neighbors?" Gabi asked, obviously surprised.

"I asked him if he still did a bunch to give away and he said 'kind of,' but not like he used to." It was hard to read what exactly was going on in Gabi's face, but it was somewhere between disbelief and affection.

"My brother's a piece of work." Gabi shook her head as she chomped on a grape. "Mami, come hear this," she yelled and a moment later Veronica walked into the kitchen.

"Que fue, mija?" the older woman asked. She had a duster in her hands, which almost made Perla laugh since the entire house was spotless. Never mind Gael also had a whole staff taking care of the cleaning. But Perla knew from experience that there was clean and then there was Caribbean people clean.

"Gael told Perla that he still 'kind of' gave desserts to the people in the neighborhood." Okay, Gael had obviously been lying.

Veronica clicked her tongue and looked at Perla with a sad smile. "My son works so hard on hiding the kind of man he really is."

"He doesn't do the flans for neighbors?"

Abuela, who had also drifted into the room, didn't give Veronica a chance to respond. "He stopped making them when his schedule got too busy, but he started a charity that provides Thanksgiving and Nochebuena meals for thousands of families. He started it just in Connecticut, but last year he expanded it and they do it in Puerto Rico, too. That boy is too humble. He won't let us tell anyone it's him."

"But why wouldn't he tell me that?" Perla asked, hurt that he didn't trust her enough to share what he'd done.

Veronica shook her head as she walked over to Perla, her brows furrowed. "Gael's been closed off for a long time."

"Mami," Gabi warned as if trying to stave off whatever her mother would do next, but Veronica waved her off.

"Dejame, Gabriela. I'm just letting Perlita know the truth. He was never the same after your relationship ended, mija." Veronica held Perla's hand in hers. "I'm glad you're back in each other's lives. Gaelito looks happier already."

"I don't know if it's just me causing that. He's so happy that you're recovered."

Veronica shook her head, a small, knowing smile on her lips. "He's very happy about that, but it's not what put a smile on his face at breakfast this morning."

Perla wanted to hide away from the hope she saw in Veronica's eyes. Not only because they were lying to everyone, but also because Perla wished more than anything that what was happening between them was real. She would pay dearly for what she started with Gael, just like she had the first time. But she would be damned if she was going to stop. She was willing to live with the fallout, whatever that was.

Twelve

"Perla, did you hear me?"

"Oh, sorry. What did you need?" She'd been distracted since she came back from the house. Some of the warmth and playfulness from the morning was replaced by aloofness.

"The Chantilly cream for the tres leches," he reminded her, pointing at the mixing bowl of snowy-white whipped cream. She handed it over distractedly as she looked out the window.

"Is something wrong? Did you hear from Carmelina?" He wasn't sure how things stood with Perla and her mother, but their relationship had always been strained. Especially around the holidays. She shook her head in response and looked up at him with those sad gray eyes.

"My mom's barely talking to me these days. She didn't take it well when I sold my shares to help Esmeralda."

"I can imagine."

He'd heard about that. It had been all over the news when Perla's half sister took over as president of the studio, and Rodrigo Almanzar, the former chief content officer, was officially appointed by the board as CEO of Sambrano. Rodrigo had a long history with the Sambranos, but it had surprised everyone when it leaked that Perla had sold her stake in the family business to him. Carmelina Sambrano, Perla's mother, was as blue blood as they came. Her very conservative Latin family owned a chain of high-end restaurants, which was now apparently in financial trouble. And it certainly would not have made her happy to lose access to her daughter's fortune in company shares.

"Do you want to talk about it?" he asked, finding it increasingly harder to see her upset and not be able to do anything about it.

"Why didn't you tell me about your charity? That you give dinners to families for the holidays?" she asked almost in an accusatory tone, her eyes flashing with something that looked like genuine hurt.

This was what had her upset? He sighed, silently cursing his sister and her big mouth. "I don't know. I didn't want you to think I was trying to impress you with my 'good deeds.'"

"Impress me? Gael, *you're* the movie star."

"That's not who I am to you, though. I'm just Gael from Bridgeport to you."

"You've never been *just* anything to me, Gael." The way she said it, like it was the last thing she wanted to come out of her mouth but she couldn't keep it inside anymore, rocked him.

"Why are you really here, Perla?" he asked, even if he knew the answer would only make things worse.

She eyed him as she worked on making caramel for the flan. "I'm here because I wanted you to take the part. I came because I remember this being the kind of role you dreamed about in college." She stopped fussing with the melted sugar and braced her hands on the counter like she was trying to find her strength for the conversation, then she hung her head for a moment. He watched as her back lifted and then slumped. Noticed how there was a tiny red bruise on her neck, which looked very much like teeth marks, and he wished he could be the man this woman deserved.

"You're the best person for the job," she said matter-of-factly, "and I could put my feelings aside and get the actor who could make the project a success or I could sulk. You're not the only one who can put business first," she added with finality as she looked him dead in the eyes.

Something bruised and feral howled inside his chest at her answer. Deep down he'd wanted her to tell him she'd come to see him, that she'd wanted to know if things between them could still work. But he couldn't blame her for protecting herself. It was the only smart thing either of them had done since she'd arrived.

"So this was purely professional. It had nothing to do with our history?" he asked, and she turned her eyes down. He wondered what the hell he was trying to accomplish rehashing all this.

"I'm not sure what you're fishing for, Gael." She sounded exasperated as she cleaned her hands on a tea towel and moved toward him. "But I can tell you this. No matter what my plan was when I got here yesterday, sleeping with you was not part of it." He swallowed hard as she came to stand right in front of him, her slight body pressed to his front. The urge to touch her made his heart punch against his chest. "And you know what?"

"What?" Speech was becoming more and more elusive with every passing second.

Her smile deepened at his one-word question, and the expression made her look thoroughly wicked. He gasped as her nails scraped the back of his neck; the jolt of sensation went straight to his groin.

"I'm not going to spend any more time hesitating. I want you." She let the words linger as she snaked a hand down to the front of his joggers and palmed his hard cock. He stiffened at the lazy stroking motion, gritting his teeth to keep from taking her right on this counter. "Mmm." Those sounds she made were going to end him. "And I think you want me." He let out a pained sound, too turned on to make words. "We have this…just for the holidays. What do you say?"

Just for the holidays.

Sure, he could say no, but he wasn't going to. Not when she was offering and he was desperate to take everything she could give him. He let his hands slide down to her backside and dug in, the denim of her jeans rough against his palms, and thrust into her hand. "I say you better stop stroking my dick, unless you want me to bend you over this kitchen island," he said through a clenched jaw.

"Mmm, that sounds hot," she answered before she licked into his mouth. After a moment she pulled back with a very wicked grin. "But later," she declared. "After dinner tonight, when we have time."

He was going to come just from that throaty laugh of hers. "You're playing with fire, Perla Sambrano," he warned as he went in for a hungry kiss. They ate at each other's mouths for a few breathless moments until they both pulled back, panting. He had to bite back a grin at the dazed expression on her face.

"I'm looking forward to being burned, Gael Montez," she said a little wobblier than just a second ago, but no less sexy. He could not wait to get this woman in his bed and wreck her completely.

"Now, let's finish this flan before another one of your family members walks in on us half-naked," she teased, and despite the extreme case of blue balls he was experiencing, he laughed.

"Family's overrated," he groused as he worked on getting his erection and his breathing under control.

She clicked her tongue, shaking her head in feigned disapproval. "You're crazy about your family," she told him with a smile that beckoned him to go back in for another kiss.

I'm crazy about you, but that's just going to leave us both in pieces like it did the last time.

"I'm almost done," Perla called from the bedroom as she finished putting on her diamond studs. She stood straight as she took in her reflection in the mirror. She was wearing a replica of a black Balenciaga gown from the 1965 winter collection. She'd bought the original dress at auction to donate to the Fashion Institute in New York, and the House of Balenciaga had offered to make her this one when they'd heard. It was a sleek and simple design in the front, with long sleeves and a knot at the waist that brought attention to the A-line skirt. But the back was what drew her to the dress. It had a deep scoop that showed a lot of skin. It made the dress sexy and elegant at the same time.

She loved vintage couture and had amassed quite a valuable collection over the years, though this one was one of her favorites. She'd intended to wear it for Nochebuena in Punta Cana but if she was honest, it was more fitting for an evening dining by a fireplace. She'd done little with her makeup—just a bit of mascara, her new trademark winged eyeliner and red lipstick.

She looked good. Healthy and elegant, but more than anything she loved how she felt in this dress. In her own skin. She ran her hands over the skirt, looking at her reflection. Her skin buzzed with anticipation. In part it was that she was looking forward to spending time with Gael's family, but mostly she couldn't stop thinking about what would happen after. All day they'd been circling each other, only to clash into frantic, breath-stealing kisses. It had always been like this for her when it came to Gael, like her body was dormant for anyone else, but with him the fire inside her roared to life in an instant. It was more than desire; it was a bone-deep wild need.

The truth was that she'd probably never stop wanting Gael. That no matter how much of him she got she'd always want more. They'd agreed that this thing they were doing could only go on until she left. And she should be glad. She'd gotten what she came to do; he'd agreed to take the role. And this time she knew what was coming. She would have time to prepare for the goodbye.

"That really doesn't make any of it better," she sighed as she stepped into her Louboutin heels. She'd have to take them off in a minute and switch into snow boots for the walk to the main house, but she wanted to see the whole outfit together. "I look kind of hot," she told herself, even if the smile from before had waned a little.

She heard a light knock on the door before it opened just a couple of inches.

"Can I come in?"

Her heart kicked up in her chest to a gallop, as butterflies fluttered in her belly from hearing Gael's voice. "Sure, come on in." He'd let her have the bedroom while he changed in the other room, so she hadn't seen him in his own Nochebuena best yet. She closed her eyes for a second, bracing herself for the sight of Gael Montez in a suit.

"Perla," he breathed out as she turned around to face him. His eyes roamed over her hungrily, and she would've flushed at the attention, but she was too busy staring at him. He was wearing a burgundy velvet jacket—which she recognized from Tom Ford's latest collection—and black slacks. His chin-length hair was parted at the center and framed his gorgeous face perfectly. The man really was movie-star handsome. Those shoulders filled out the jacket perfectly and her hands itched to touch him. And lucky for her there was nothing and no one stopping her from doing it all night.

"You look amazing," he told her as he came closer. Without hesitation he took her in his arms and kissed her cheek. "Tan bella." No one had ever called her beautiful before Gael. Or maybe they had, but with him it was the first time she'd believed it. Because there was no way to mistake what she saw in his eyes when he looked at her. The mix of tenderness and barely contained hunger with which he touched her. It was why it had been such a shock when he'd ended things. But that was not relevant now, not when Gael was holding her like she was everything he needed.

"I have something for you," he whispered in her ear, bringing her focus back to him.

"You do?" She could hear the smile in her voice and goodness, how was that possible after knowing everything she knew? After the heartache. After so much time. How could this man still turn her inside out? She felt him reach into his pocket and then he brought a hand up to show her. In his palm was a pair of pearl drop earrings.

"Where did you get this?" she asked as she plucked one out of his hand. It was clearly vintage, done in an Art-Deco style. The perfect tear-shaped pearl dangled from a row of baguette-cut diamonds, and at the top was a perfect round-cut ruby encircled by tiny diamonds. When she turned it around, she saw the Cartier stamp along the clasp.

"Do you like them?" She just looked up at him, too stunned to do anything but shake her head. *Like them?* If he would've given her hundreds of earrings to choose from, these would've been the ones she'd pick.

"I love them," she told him as she moved to take off the ones she was wearing, so she could put the new ones on. "Seriously, though, where did you get them?"

He grinned at her, having a little too much fun with his vintage jewelry prowess. "Remember when I slipped out while you were helping set the table?"

"Yes…" The rest of what she was going to say died in her throat as he moved to help her put on the earrings.

"Our next-door neighbor owns an antique jewelry store in town. She usually has some pieces at home," he informed her as he nimbly hooked an earring on one side and then the other. "There," he told her before pressing a kiss on her cheek and stepping back to look at her. Good grief. It was like he could tell whenever she'd managed to convince herself she could walk away from this unscathed, and then intentionally said or did something to remind her she was fooling herself.

"Perfect." The way he said it sounded like he wasn't just referring to the earrings, but she was not reckless enough to assume he was talking about them. Without saying a word she let him put his hands on her shoulders and move her until she was facing the mirror again.

"Gael," she said, too afraid of what would come out of her mouth to risk another word. He was right; they were perfect. The ideal complement to her gown. He was standing right behind her, and even in her heels he towered over her. He ran his hands possessively over her flanks, waist and hips.

"I can't stop thinking about tonight," he whispered hotly against her ear, and she had to bite down not to moan. "As soon as we come back tonight, I'm going to take off this dress and put my mouth right here." He placed the heel of his hand right at the apex of her thighs, and pressed hard.

"Ah," Perla gasped, and her head lolled on his shoulder. The lids of her eyes felt heavy and she lowered them until she could barely see through. It was thrilling to look at them both in the mirror while he touched her like this. "We need to go to dinner soon," she said in a reedy voice she could hardly recognize.

"We will, but as soon as we're back here I'm going to have you screaming for me, Perla. I'm going to lick and taste you until you come on my tongue, and then I'm going to take my sweet time with you." He punctuated each word with a roll of his hips, letting her feel exactly what it was that he was going to give her. This was them, always. Sweet and sinful all at once, a perfect match. They *looked* perfect, too. Elegant, young and perfect. Like they belonged together. That thought went a long way to suffuse the fire roiling in her blood, and she smiled sadly at the picture they made. She turned to look up at him and for a second she thought she saw a flash of her own regret in his eyes.

She turned her back on the reflection of everything she wanted and could not have. "I'm ready," she told him without daring to look in his eyes again.

He looked at her for a second, as if there was something he wanted to tell her. But after a moment he shook his head and smiled. "Are you sure you're ready for the madness of Nochebuena with the Montezes?"

"More than ready," she assured him, ignoring the stab of longing she felt. And the truth was she did look forward to this evening, and all that it would entail. Fake or not, this was the closest thing to real happiness she'd felt in a while. She wouldn't waste a moment of it. Life would come calling soon enough.

Thirteen

"Let me help with that, Veronica."

Gael grinned as he found Perla gently coaxing his mother to stop taking dishes to the kitchen. They'd finished dinner moments ago and despite there being staff to help with the cleaning, his mother and grandmother could not quite relax.

"Mami, listen to Perla," he said as he wrapped his arms around his mother's thin shoulders while winking at his fake girlfriend. Although nothing about the way he'd been feeling about Perla felt anywhere near fake.

"Ay, Gael, I'm fine," his mother groused as he nudged her out of the kitchen.

"I know you're fine, but you've also been cooking all day since you refused to let the chef help you."

"I like to make my family's Nochebuena dinner myself." He grinned at his mother's stubbornness.

"And we appreciate your efforts. That arroz con gandules was really the best I've ever had," Perla interjected as she joined them.

"See, this is why I like you better than my kids. You always know what to say," Veronica teased as she leaned to place a hand on Perla's cheek. "We're so happy to have you here with us this year, Perlita. I hope we get you for many more Nochebuenas." Guilt pierced Gael's chest, and right underneath that he felt the undeniable yearning that his mother's words evoked. No matter how much he knew things with Perla could never work, he still wanted her forever. Especially now when she was moving around their house like she belonged here. When he could barely keep it together, knowing what awaited them once they were alone. But he was still a Montez, and no matter how hard he tried he would end up breaking her heart.

"Ay, mi canción," his mother squealed, bringing both Perla and his attention to the older woman. "Ven, Gaelito, take your mother out on the dance floor for a song or two. You know I can't sit still when El Gran Combo is playing."

"You heard your mother, Gael. A bailar." Perla fluttered her hands in the direction of the clearing in the living room.

He resisted the urge to pull her hand and bring her in for a kiss and did as he was told. When he and his mother were moving around the living room, dancing to the old salsa classic, he couldn't help looking back in Perla's direction.

"Your uncle has been trying to call you. He said that you hadn't picked up the phone." The mention of Manolo was a bucket of cold water on his fevered thoughts about Perla.

"We've talked twice already, and I have nothing more to say to him right now." Gael sighed, causing his mother to raise an eyebrow in question.

"What's going on, mijo?"

Manolo was supposed to come back for Nochebuena, but the same snowstorm that stranded Perla with them ended up keeping his uncle in the city. And even if he'd never tell his mother, he was glad his uncle hadn't been here to interfere with this decision about the Rios project. He suppressed another sigh as his mother scrutinized whatever she was seeing in his face. "Is something going on with you two?"

"Tio doesn't want me to take the project Perla's studio is producing." His mother pursed her lips at that but didn't interrupt. "He thinks it will hurt my career to pigeonhole me by playing such a 'Latinx' role."

She scoffed at that, making Gael grin. "And since when does Manolo know better than you do where you can take your career?" His mother was a beautiful dancer and could move to the music instinctually, so she had no problem having a serious conversation and keeping to the beat.

"Manolo has been a good manager. I take his advice seriously. And for the most part it hasn't led me astray." He admitted this because it was the truth, mostly. No one knew about the advice Manolo had given Gael about Perla six years ago. He never told his mother, not even when she rebuked Gael for "breaking that sweet girl's heart," that it had been Manolo pressuring him that pushed him to end things.

His mother was sentimental and would've seen the decision as mercenary. But Gael had understood Manolo's reasoning. He'd been on the rise, and the media loved an eligible bachelor. His career had sky-rocketed after the news got out that he was single. It had made sense at the time, but it was undeniable that the cost turned out to be much higher than he'd imagined.

"Manolo has been good to us, that's true," his mother said, bringing him out of his thoughts. "But you have made him a very rich man, son." His mother raised her hand to caress his cheek and gave a regretful little shake of the head. "He stepped in to be a father figure to you when Gabriel left, but he did that *by choice*. Besides, that's my debt to Manolo, not yours."

People saw his mother and her gentle demeanor and didn't realize there was a lioness hidden inside her. He owed everything he was to this woman. But even if she was right about not being beholden to Manolo, things were still complicated when it came to him and Perla.

"Mami, even if I take the role—"

"If?" his mother asked, making him laugh.

"Okay, mujer. Fine. I have decided to take the role, but that still doesn't mean things between Perla and me are fine. I don't—"

"You don't what?" Telling his mother he was certain he'd hurt Perla would not go over well, since the woman was convinced both her children were angels. But not even she couldn't deny that his lifestyle didn't exactly allow for relationships. And it was probably smart to start planting the seed that Perla would not be a permanent addition to family gatherings, even if the very thought of that hit him like a punch to the gut.

"I don't know if I can be the type of person Perla needs for the long run," he said, and his eyes instinctually scanned the room, searching for the woman in question, until he found her. As if she could sense him looking at her, she turned around and smiled at him. The effect of those gray eyes on him was forceful and absolute. He would never want anything like he wanted Perla Sambrano.

"I like how you look at her. And I *love* the way she looks at you. I can tell she sees in you the same thing I do."

"And what's that, Mami?" he asked, unable to help himself.

"A good man. A good son. A good brother. A keeper," his mother told him happily. And his gut clenched at the reckoning he knew was coming.

"How do *I* look at her?" he asked, eager to keep

hearing what his mother saw between them, as if that wouldn't just make all this worse later.

"With fire in your eyes, querido. You always did, and that passion has been gone since you two split up." His mother clicked her tongue, head shaking as if the situation had been a very sorry one indeed. "I know you love your job, and what a blessing it is that the world sees and values your gift. You're a wonder, my son, so remarkable." Sadness moved through her face from whatever she was recalling. "But I know you're not happy. I know you said you'd both decided to end it, but I knew you still had feelings for her and now I see it. The light is back in your eyes."

"I'm happy because you're healthy again, Mami," he assured her.

"I know you are," she told him, squeezing the hand he was holding as he led her across the dance floor. "But maybe now that I'm doing better you'll be a little selfish and focus on your woman. And I don't care what Manolo says. You do whatever you want to do. If he doesn't like it, too bad."

"Mami...you're being pushy," he warned as a surge of possessiveness coursed through him at the words *your woman*.

"Looks like someone wants to give you some competition," his mother quipped and he turned his head to watch Perla getting pulled onto the dance floor by the son of one of their neighbors. Since they lived in one of the most exclusive zip codes in the country everyone at their little Nochebuena dinner after-party was loaded, and it seemed like Perla had garnered the attention of the heir to a Latinx fashion empire. Miguel Correa was a little older than Gael, but undisputedly handsome, and he was looking at Gael's fake girlfriend like he wanted to swallow her whole. Gael's eyes zeroed in on the spot on Perla's wrist where Miguel had placed his hand and made a menacing sound. He wanted to go and physically remove him from her vicinity.

His mother's knowing laugh pulled him out of his bloodthirsty thoughts. "You're absolutely not allowed to rip our guests arms out, mijo."

If Miguel didn't stop with the touching and close-talking, he would be lucky if his arm was all he lost.

"Why don't you go rescue her and I'll go talk to Gabi and Abuela? We should be wrapping up soon. Your vieja can't party like she used to." His mother's joke went a long way to cool off his fury, but after giving her a kiss and walking her over to the couch where Gabi and Abuela were observing the proceedings, he went right back to glaring at Perla and her suitor.

"Bendito, bro, are you going to let Miguel outdo you like that?" Gabi teased like the smart-ass she was, and Gael had to make an effort not to grind his molars to dust as he watched the man glide through their living room with Perla. Blood rushed to his head as a choir of "mine, mine, mine" rang through his head.

"I'll be back in a minute."

"Go get her, tiger." His sister was such a pain in the ass.

Gael moved purposefully the few yards to the

middle of the room. Perla danced gracefully, her hips swaying to an old-school merengue. Miguel was giving it his all, moving his feet with perfect form, but Perla seemed distracted, her eyes roaming the room until they landed on him, and her whole face lit up.

And damn, Gael was in so much trouble. He had no idea how he was supposed to walk away from this. The way her eyes roamed over him made his heart claw at the inside of his chest. As he reached her he took one long breath in through his nose and let it out slowly before he opened his mouth, trying to calm the storm brewing inside him. How could he still want her this much? How could he let her go?

"May I interrupt?" he asked after unclenching his teeth, his heavy hand on one of Miguel's shoulders. Miguel did a double take at whatever he saw in Gael's face, and immediately let go of Perla.

"Your girl can dance, man. If you don't watch out I might try to steal her from you."

I'd love to see you try, asshole.

Gael bared his teeth in answer and slid his arm around's Perla's waist. Within seconds he'd taken his woman as far away from Miguel Correa's greasy hands as he could.

Perla shook her head and laughed as he started moving them around the room. "Well, this is not a very flattering side of you," she told him, but her eyes were twinkling.

"You love it." He was practically growling, and she threw her head back and laughed in earnest.

"I wouldn't say *love*," she told him with a wink.

"But it's kind of flattering to see you drop your stoic mask for a bit. I've always liked it when you let your passions run wild, Gael."

And that was where this woman would end him. The way she let him see everything. Unafraid to show him that he'd pleased her. He'd been in Hollywood for so long he'd forgotten what it was like to have someone who didn't pretend. Who said what she meant and meant what she said. Someone who despite the ways she'd been hurt—*hurt by him*—could still be this open.

The song changed from a faster tempo merengue to "Veinte Años," a slow, moody bolero about a story of a twenty-year-old love affair that cannot be forgotten. Because his sister was in charge of the music and she loved messing with his head. But as Perla melted into his arms, he pressed her to him and let himself have this moment. For so long he'd refused to dwell in his feelings and when a light had gone out inside him, he'd told himself it was for the best. That he didn't have time for love; he had responsibilities. His entire family was depending on him. And until this moment, he hadn't permitted himself to admit that breaking up with Perla had carved out a piece of his soul and it had never grown back.

"Are my moves not to your liking or do you just enjoy scowling?" Perla asked jokingly, looking up at him. Her cheeks were flushed from dancing. She looked so beautiful. And her moves were more than to his liking. He had a hand on her hip and could feel them sway seductively to the music. Unbidden a memory of her astride him, rocking with him in that same sensual rhythm, robbed him of breath. Suddenly, he couldn't wait any longer; all he wanted was to drag her out of that room and finish what they'd started that morning.

"You know your dancing is fire," he told her and laughed when she made a show of fanning herself at his compliment. God, this woman—he didn't just find her irresistible, he also liked her. He liked her so damn much. Impulsively, he bent down to press a kiss to her mouth. As expected, there was a flurry of cheers and whistles coming from where his family was sitting, but he couldn't even be bothered to care. He wanted every person in this room to see how much he wanted Perla Sambrano.

He pressed his fingers into her skin until she was flush against him, and every nerve in his body buzzed with electricity. They were still clutching hands, and he squeezed her tighter. Needing to ground them both in this kiss. He tasted her gently, a sharing of breath that seemed to fill his lungs with oxygen. He imagined their hearts speeding up in unison as he deepened the caress. He was wondering how much longer they'd have to stay at the party before he took her back to the cottage, when something buzzed against his leg and almost instantly Perla stiffened.

She pulled back, the haziness in her eyes gone, replaced by uncomfortable alertness. That was when he heard the faint ringtone. It sounded like a horn of some sort.

"Is that your phone?" he asked curiously as she unclenched her hand from his and slid it in the pocket of her dress.

"It's my mom," she whispered with a grimace and she signaled to the hallway at the other end of the room that led to the den. "I've been avoiding her all day." He nodded and made a move to follow her, feeling protective. He suspected her mother was probably calling just to ruin her evening, and he didn't want to leave her to face it all alone. Then he reminded herself that no matter what his dick or his family thought about the situation, he was not actually her man. Not in any way that gave him the right to walk out of this room with her or intrude in a private conversation.

And thankfully, she had her head on straight better than he did, because she slipped out of his hands with the phone pressed to her ear and walked out of the room without a single glance in his direction.

Fourteen

"Are you okay?" he asked again as they walked into the cottage.

"You know how my mother is," she told him in a brittle, subdued voice as she worked to take off her coat and boots. Her mother could always do that to Perla, suck the joy right out of her. He'd seen it so many times when they were together. Perla would take her mother's call glowing and happy and after a two-minute conversation, she'd walk back into the room ashen and looking a little lost. Carmelina's poisonous words always struck true; a few well-aimed barbs and she could incinerate Perla's happiness down to ashes.

"I'm sorry," he said, biting back angry words. She didn't need to hear what he thought about her mother.

That would only hurt Perla, and Carmelina had taken enough from her already. If she was his, he'd make sure she never…no, there was no point going there. She had already been his and he'd squandered her love, just like her family had, and she deserved so much better than that, from everyone in her life.

"I don't want to think about her anymore," Perla said as if she could read his mind.

He knew all too well what it was like to have a parent who made you feel like shit. But his father at least had the decency to stay out of his life. Perla's mother on the other hand—despite acting like she couldn't stand her children—seemed unable to stay out of their lives.

He hated how resigned she seemed to always fall short in her mother's eyes, how it still hurt her. He knew he couldn't spare her that. But he could make her feel good. Tonight, if she let him, he would worship her. Show her with his body and his hands that every inch of her was precious to him.

"Here, let me help you." He quickly took his own coat off and reached for Perla as she attempted to slide out of hers. He carefully pulled it off her arms, and she shivered as the air hit her bare shoulders and back. He couldn't help staring at the lines of her. He could write poetry about the way her soft curves felt under the palm of his hand. About the feel of her skin on his lips. The hunger she awakened in him.

He hung her coat on a hook and moved to stand behind her. He rubbed his hands together before placing them on her shoulders and bent down to kiss the nape of her neck. "You looked beautiful tonight," he whispered against her warm skin, making her tremble in his arms. He loved this new style of hers. Vampy and a little mysterious. Made him want to discover all the things about her that he'd been too afraid to explore before. He'd suspected it six years ago and he was certain of it now. He could spend his life discovering this woman, finding a million different ways to make her feel loved. To make her believe that she was every inch as valuable as her name.

A pearl. A treasure.

He kept kissing her as she swayed in his arms. Pressing his lips down her neck and over to her shoulders. Pausing to take in her smell, greedily tasting her velvety skin. He wanted to consume her. He'd been getting nibbles when what he wanted was to feast on her. Take his time with every delectable part of her body he hadn't yet tended to.

"Your hands feel like heaven," she said in a breathy, low voice, like warm honey.

"I want you," he confessed against her ear as his fingers worked on undoing the small buttons at the back of her gown.

"I want you, too. So much," Perla gasped, brushing her ass against his hard cock. His hands shook with the need to possess her. He fought for control as he slowly revealed more of her skin. She'd gone without a bra since the back of the dress was so low. The thought of those brown peaks brushing against the soft material of her gown made him go impossibly harder.

"Perfect," he said as he helped her step out of it. A primal noise rumbled in his chest as his hands slid down her back to the lacy edge of her panties. The black lace covered very little and it framed her delicious backside in a way that made his mouth water.

"What do you want?" he asked, holding himself back. He needed to ask if he was allowed to touch, because once he started he wasn't stopping until there wasn't a single inch of her left for him to savor.

"You," she told him, and he wished he could give her all of him, forever. But they had tonight. Every ounce of his focus, every second of his attention, would be for her. Without hesitation he scooped her up, eliciting a surprised little squeal out of her. But she didn't fight him; she just wrapped her arms around his neck and let him take her to the bedroom.

He was fully dressed, but for his shoes, and there was something carnal and raw about having her almost naked in his arms. He bent his head, seeking her mouth, and licked into her as he placed her down on the edge of the bed. He knelt between her spread thighs and took her in. With this woman in front of him like this, open and ready for him, Gael imagined himself on the edge of a crossroad that could take his life on a completely different path. One he could not come back from. Like every step forward would burn what he left behind.

He looked up at pert breasts lifting and descending with her quick breaths. Her mouth was swollen from his kisses, the embodiment of everything he'd ever wanted.

"Perla." Her name was a commandment, a calling. A vow he would surely break. "Show me where you want me to touch you," he demanded, and smiled when a flush of pink appeared on the apples of her cheeks.

His sweet Perla. She looked so different now than the girl he'd known. Her hair, her clothes, her body. She was more luscious now, grown. And yet, that shyness, that untainted pureness, was still there.

"Here," she said and followed the command by palming her breast with one hand, and with the other she slid her panties down and off. Gael felt like all the air left his lungs at once. "Make love to me."

"Are you sure?" he asked as his cock turned to granite in his briefs.

"I've missed you," she said, simply. No games. Just the truth. Then she turned those gray eyes on him. Like rolling clouds before a storm. "And don't act like I'm a delicate flower. I may not have done this in a while, but I do know how bad I want this."

"You're going to kill me," he said in a hoarse, taut voice as he ran the pads of his thumbs over her pussy. Her confession of not having sex with anyone else after they broke up should have made him feel like the worst kind of bastard, but his chest pulsed with the knowledge that he was still the only man to have ever been inside her. That when he entered her, he'd be the only one to ever fill her up. The only one to move inside her while she shattered in his arms. That no other man had felt the hot, delicious grip of her body. He let his hands roam over the silky skin of her legs, pressed his palms to the inside of her thighs so he could spread her for his view. He sucked in a breath when he saw the brown-and-pink dewy petals at her core.

"Gorgeous." He looked up, already licking his lips in anticipation for her taste. "I'm starving for you."

"Then consume me, Gael," she demanded like an empress as she leaned back on her hands, her half-closed eyes focused on him. Without taking his gaze off her he brought one hand up to her breasts and pulled on the hard, brown tips.

"Ah," she moaned, and arched her back to give him more access. And because he couldn't help himself he lifted his mouth until he could suck on her nipples. He lazily circled one areola and the other, then ran the flat of his tongue between her breasts before returning to the place he craved.

He nudged her legs open and pressed his nose to the furrow of her labia. "I'm going to lick you. Circle this sweet little *pearl* with my tongue until you come."

She laughed, a husky sensual laugh that made his dick pulse painfully in his slacks. He started with one long and slow lick with the flat of his tongue, which rewarded him with breathy little moans. "Suck on your fingers, babe," he instructed her. "Play with your clit while I taste your honey. Show me how you make yourself come when you're on your own."

His head felt hot as she watched her do exactly as he asked her. She lifted one hand and inserted three fingers into her mouth. Sucked on them for a few seconds and swirled her tongue around them.

"Fuck, that's hot," he muttered, lips right against her heat before he speared her with his tongue. Her sweetness flooded his senses and he almost came on the spot. He lapped at her a few more times before he made himself stop. He grabbed her wrist and brought her wet fingers to her pussy. "Show me."

"Bossy," she panted as a wicked grin pulled up her lips. This woman didn't stop surprising him. There was this untarnished purity to her, but she had a fire inside that could burn him to ashes. Gael had forced himself to forget how it had been with her. The way she ignited his blood every time they were together. The way that for him she was an incandescent flame no one else got to see. She always gave him everything. That was why no one since had ever come close. No one could undo him like Perla could.

"Keep going, amor," he urged her, and she brought the pads of her fingers to her heat and touched herself. First, two fingers rubbing on her clitoris, then three. She circled them fast, spreading her legs wider.

"You're so close," he groaned as his dick pulsed in his pants.

"Yes," she panted as she pumped two fingers inside herself, and he had to taste her. He spread her labia and put his mouth on her. She moaned low, rolling her hips into his mouth, and soon her legs were trembling as an orgasm washed over her.

He was going to die if he didn't get inside her soon. He lapped and sucked at her a few more times while she lay on her back, sated and so beautiful it almost hurt to look at her. He made quick work of his clothes and soon he was kneeling between her thighs. He took a moment to admire the wild beauty on his bed. The woman whom he'd been telling himself for so long he couldn't love. And what empty, cowardly lies those had been. He was *full* of love for her, and even if that meant having to let her go, he would not waste what she was offering him.

"Mmm." She pushed into his touch as he slid the palms of his hands over her. First, her calves, then up her legs, the inside of her thighs. He pressed the heel of his hand to her core, making her suck in a breath. He gripped her hips and caressed the softness of her belly, pressing his lips at her navel. He cupped her breasts and pinched her nipples, making her arch for him.

"You're so beautiful," he told her as he touched her. He bent down and kissed her, her taste still on his tongue. He felt her hands on his shoulders, on his back, and it was like his skin was coming back to life. Each caress woke up a part of him that had been asleep for far too long.

He pulled back for a second and hovered over her. "Hi," she told him through a smile, and he felt his heart crack a little from how sweet she was. How would he ever walk away from this?

"When do I get to see if you still have the magic touch?" Perla asked as she stroked Gael. She felt him shiver as she squeezed on the head of his penis.

"Very, very soon," he promised her, and made his

way down her body. Her first orgasm had already been so intense that she feared she'd be too sensitive, but as soon as he touched, she instinctively spread her legs wide to give him more access. Gael's hands were a marvel. Gentle and rough at once. His fingertips could flutter over her skin like butterfly wings one moment and the next roughly bring her to her climax. If this wasn't so good, she'd almost regret doing it. Because she *knew* the descent would be grim. Losing him the last time had been almost unbearable, and she knew this time it would be worse. He hadn't made her any promises beyond this day, but how she wished this man could be hers forever.

"Oh," she gasped as she felt slick fingers at her vulva. She'd seen him grab the lube and now she felt the slippery gel as he applied it on her. He smoothly slid two fingers in, then flipped his hand so that he could massage that spot inside that made her tremble. "Mmm...right there, Gael."

"You love that," he purred as his hands expertly caressed her. "You're so wet and hot, clenching my fingers. So tight. I can't wait to be inside you."

"Can we test that theory soon?" she panted as he did something delicious to her with his thumbs. "Please."

"Since you asked so nicely." She opened her eyes and found that his face was a lot more serious than his words had been. She looked down her body and saw that he was rolling on a condom. Perla raised her knees so he could see that she welcomed this. More than welcomed—she burned for him. Had dreamt about this moment so many times, it almost felt surreal. And even if Gael would never be hers again, right now the only thing that mattered was having him inside her. After coating himself with lube he put a pillow under her hips, and soon the tip of his cock was nudging at her entrance.

"Are you ready for me, sweetheart?" His eyes were wide open and the way his lips tugged up into a sexy smile made all the air rush out of her lungs. The way he touched her would be what she'd always remember from this night *and she would remember*. The intensity of his gaze, the raw need, was electrifying. To know she made this strong, beautiful man—whom millions of women thought of as the perfect male specimen—tremble with desire was overwhelming.

"Wrap your legs around me," he demanded as he pushed in. He gritted his teeth as he entered her with excruciating patience until he was in to the hilt. She felt so full, like he was inside her and around her.

"How does it feel?" he asked tautly.

"Like it's almost too much. Like you're stretching me all the way to the edge before pain but, instead of less of you, I want more," she confessed.

"God, the things you say, baby," he said and shuddered out a breath, and his face twisted in what looked like a mix of agony and ecstasy. "This is so sweet." He was moving in her now and when he thrust in she felt a tightness and then a moment of real pain; it had been a very long time since she'd done this.

He looked down at her, face full of concern. "Do you need me to stop? I can pull out—"

She tightened her legs around him and shook her head. "Don't you dare, Gael Montez. I've waited too long for this. I just need a moment."

"Okay," he said before pressing his lips to hers. He tipped her in a way that made her feel full to the brim. He rolled his hips into her and she met him stroke for stroke until the burning stretch turned into something languid and delicious.

She gasped when he pulled out and flipped her onto her stomach and then entered her again from behind. His hands pinched her breasts as he surged into her, making her cry out with mindless pleasure. Then, like he could read her thoughts, he brought his hand down and stroked her clit as he took her hard. Within moments she was crying out her orgasm and he followed her a moment later. His gasp of tortured pleasure, hot against her ear.

He held her to him for a few moments, their bodies still joined. He kissed her gently, her sweaty brow, her cheeks, and as he left her body he trailed kissed down her spine. "Thank you," he whispered so low she thought she imagined it.

She almost thanked him, too, but she didn't want to shatter the moment with words. Morning and reality were coming and she wanted to keep this perfect cocoon they'd built around them for as long as she could.

"Regrets?" he asked her as he ran a warm washcloth between her legs. Caring for her in a way that made her almost want to weep. He'd tried to sound neutral but she could see a wariness in his gorgeous eyes.

She shook her head and told him the truth. "Not a single one. It was worth the wait." *You were worth the wait.*

Fifteen

"Feliz Navidad, cariño," Gael whispered in Perla's ear and yeah, this was a far superior Christmas morning wake-up than any she'd had in recent memory.

"Mmm…good morning," she said as she stretched languidly in his arms. She was deliciously naked under layers of fluffy warm blankets and quite literally wrapped up in the man who had owned her heart since she was nineteen. She wanted to hold on to this feeling forever.

Gael rolled his hips into her, his hardness pressing into her backside, and just like that she was burning for him again.

"Someone has a special gift for me," she teased as his hands roamed over her.

"I do," he whispered hotly in her ear, while his hands plucked the tips of her breasts.

"Ah," she gasped as he touched her while he slid a muscular thigh between her legs until she was open to him. "Gael, please." She had no idea what she was begging for; she just knew she ached for more of him. She needed him to make every thought evaporate from her mind.

"Mmm...I love it when you get like this." His voice in her ear was as languorous as his hands on her body. He slowly slid one down her torso until he was at the hot center of her. He palmed her there, and she pressed into his touch. One of his fingers slid into her, and she instinctively tightened around him. "I love how you feel, so wet." He sounded drunk with lust, and that only ignited her own desire further, until it was bubbling like boiling water under her skin. She made a desperate sound as he pushed a second finger in while circling her clitoris with his thumb. She was so open to him, completely at his mercy. His big body enveloping her as his hands pleasured her. Her orgasm was a frenzied, frantic force that rocked through her.

"Gael!" She screamed his name until she was hoarse and still he kept touching her, coaxing more and more sensation out of her until she was limp in his arms.

"You're an excellent Christmas present," Gael told her as he peppered kisses on her neck. He'd moved them so she was sitting against him, and it was pretty perfect.

"You're not too bad yourself, Mr. Montez." She pressed into the erection that was still hot and hard and looked up at him. "Are we going to take care of this?"

"Later," he said, putting his arms around her. "That was just for you."

"Are you trying to ruin me?" Perla asked, not entirely joking, eliciting a wounded grunt from Gael. She wished she could tell him that these past two days had made it perfectly clear why she never seemed to get past the first date with anyone else. Because he was *it* for her. A man with a hard body and clever hands was not all that hard to find. But someone who could own her body and her heart, *that* she'd only ever had with this man. Perla looked out the window and saw the bright blue sky that promised a clear, sunny day, and her heart fell. She'd have to leave him soon. She had so much more than she used to when it came to family and a support system, and yet she knew she'd feel his absence like a dark, gaping void.

"Looks like it should be safe for me to drive back today," she told him, even as she tightened her arms over his. Forcing him to hold her closer.

"Hmm." She felt the rumbling in his chest as he worked on what to say to her. "You could stay here with us." Everything in her wanted to jump on that offer. The temptation to ignore the outside world and lose herself in this man and in his family was hard to resist. But this didn't belong to her. It was a mirage. She couldn't have any of it. He'd made that clear, and the longer she stayed the harder it would be to walk away.

"My sister's waiting for me and I've imposed on your family time long enough."

"Perla." He sounded reproachful, as if she'd said something egregious. "My mother has spent the last day and a half telling you that you're her Christmas miracle."

She laughed at his grumpiness, but she couldn't let him talk her into staying. This was about self-preservation. And as if the universe was in total agreement that she needed an exit plan, her phone started ringing.

"Leave it," Gael said as he did delicious things to her neck, but as tempting as he was, she needed to start drifting back to her life.

"I can't. It could be about the flight." She leaned to grab the phone and confirmed she'd been right. It was from the crew. A thirty-second exchange informed her they'd been cleared to fly, and her private flight to Punta Cana would be departing the next morning. Needing a second to push down the disappointment and despair threatening to flood her at the thought of leaving Gael, she distracted herself with texting her sister.

Perla: All set for tomorrow. I'll be there in the early afternoon. Will send details when I'm on the plane.

"Sounds like I'll be trading chilly snow for sandy beaches." For the life of her she could not make herself sound enthused about it and that only made Perla even more annoyed at herself. Because this had never been the plan. She should've already been in the DR with her family. Jumping in bed with Gael was just the cherry on top of the cake of bad choices of the last forty-eight hours. And yet, she didn't regret any of it, not when he felt so solid and warm, not when he wrapped his strong arms around her and, without a word, soothed her frayed nerves.

"What are we going to do?" she asked. He grunted, then pressed a kiss to her temple. "I think you already know the answer to that question."

It was on the tip of her tongue to say she had no clue what he was talking about, but her heart seemed to catch on before she did, racing in response to his words. Not just what he said, but *how* he said it. There was determination there. A conviction. Like he was ready to make promises.

"I'm not sure—"

"Yes, you are. You're sure, like I'm sure."

She stopped talking when he started moving, sliding out from behind her until he was standing in front of her next to the bed. And yeah, there was no way she could focus with Gael Montez in his full naked glory.

"*I'm* sure?" she asked, the question more for herself than for him.

"I think you are," he told her as he wrapped a gentle hand around her throat and tipped her face up to look at him. He was smiling pleasantly enough, but his eyes looked like they were working at boring right through her skull. "I'm not ready to close the door on what's happening here," he said as he waved a hand in the space between them. "I'm not sure what it'll look like, but I can't just let you drive out of my life."

He was deadly serious now. But she could see the hesitation in his eyes. He didn't know how any of this could work, not any more than she did. The difference was that right under his uncertainty she saw determination. He was willing to make this work.

"What does that mean?" she asked as anticipation, hope, lust and...love swirled inside her like the most intoxicating of cocktails.

"It means I finally understand that I was walking around with a giant piece of my heart missing." Oh, God, what was he doing? "The way that you walked in here yesterday, with your head high, you're so strong, baby. I don't deserve this second chance, but I want to try and earn it." She could see his throat working, and his eyes were shining with something that looked a lot like...no, she wasn't even going to think it.

"Perla, you were the first amazing thing that ever happened to me, and you are still the best. I can't give you up." She had no words, but she didn't need them because he pulled her to him, and for a moment, bent down to press their foreheads together. They took a few breaths in unison, letting the things he'd said sit between them. "I want to drive into the city with you. I..." He heaved a sigh, and she could feel the urgency rolling off him. "I want to spend tonight with you, just us. And I want to talk about how to keep seeing each other. And then you'll go to the DR and I'll go do my press tour in Asia and we'll have a lot of phone sex for those two weeks. Then I'm going to kidnap you and take you to Hawaii for a week and we'll do nothing but stay in bed and eat seafood on the beach."

He was saying everything she wanted to hear, and she wished she could just snatch what he was offering. No questions, no doubt, but she was not the girl who'd trusted blindly in the love he had for her. She knew all too well how life could get between two people, no matter how much they loved each other.

"You don't know how many times I dreamed of hearing you say this," she told him honestly as he distractingly ran his thumb over her bottom lip. "But nothing's changed in the last two days, Gael. You're the same. I'm the same, and we'd agreed that it was too complicated."

He didn't shake his head, or even contradict her for a long moment. "That's the thing, though. Everything seems to be the same, but I *feel* different, and I see you now, here in my bed, with my marks on you." He brushed two fingers over a little sore spot on her collarbone where he'd left a love bite. "And you look different to me, too. I know you feel it," he said with certainty, and bent down to kiss her. It was bruising and thorough, like he was trying to make his final argument with the kiss itself. Like them together was all the evidence he needed to show her just how different everything was. He pulled back, leaving her panting, and she knew before she said it that she'd let herself believe in everything he was offering her, even if she was certain life would undo it all in the end.

"Okay," she whispered as she gripped the hand on her neck and pulled it so he was standing between her legs. His groin was just inches away and her mouth was practically watering from the need to taste him. She fisted the base of his erection as she looked up at him. She searched his face for something, a sign that told her that trusting him was a stupid idea, but all she saw was the same lust burning through every ounce of her resistance.

"You have plans for that?" Gael asked roughly, through clenched teeth as she flicked the head with the tip of her tongue.

"Maybe. You have any ideas?"

He grunted and pushed in. "Let me in, baby," he coaxed her and she did, hungry for him again… before long all her doubts were floating away in the deep, tumultuous waters of her love for Gael Montez.

"Manolo, I can't do this right now," Gael told his uncle as he struggled to keep his voice down.

"You don't have five minutes to discuss the terms of a project you accepted without consulting me?"

Gael gritted his teeth at Manolo's reproaching tone. His uncle insisted on treating him like he was still a kid, and he was done with this shit. His mother was right. Manolo made a very good living off Gael's work and he was done acting like the old man did this as a favor to him.

Gael walked over to the window in the study and watched as two workers plowed the driveway and the path to the main road. Some days he could hardly believe he owned all this. But he'd have to start reminding himself—and his uncle—who was really running the show here.

"Manolo, let's get something straight. You're my uncle and I love you. But *you* work for *me*." He heard the older man suck in a breath, but Gael wasn't tiptoeing around Manolo's fragile ego today. "I'm taking the Francisco Rios part because it's what I want to do. End of discussion."

"And what am I supposed to tell the other studio about the lead role for that superhero franchise, Gael? I gave them my word." Manolo's voice rose on that last part, and that only worked to infuriate Gael even more.

"If you made promises on my behalf, then it's your problem how you rectify it."

"It's that girl, isn't it? You were never able to think straight when she was in the picture. Getting dicked around just like your father—"

"Manolo," Gael roared into the phone. "I suggest you rethink whatever it is you were about to say. And you better get used to seeing Perla around again."

"What does that mean?" his uncle scoffed.

"I need to go. We're about to head into Manhattan," Gael said when he heard a light knock on the door, and saw a raven-haired head pop inside. His body instantly reacted to her presence. Good God, he needed to get a grip.

"What do you mean, Manhattan? And who's *we*? I'm on my way to Sagaponack to talk to you and you're taking off?"

"I won't be here when you get in," he told his uncle as he gestured for Perla to come in. "Drive safely, Manolo."

Perla's eyes widened as she heard the name, but Gael waved off her concern.

"Is everything okay?" she asked, worry clear in her voice. He hated that he'd never stood up for her back when Manolo acted like her presence was an imposition. Once things between them were settled and he came back from his press tour, he'd really have to reconsider if it was in his career's best interest to keep him as his manager. But right now it was all about Perla and him. Everything else could wait.

"Nothing," he told her as he brought her closer. "Just checking in. Looks like the contract for the Rios project came in yesterday."

She smiled up at him when she heard that. "I told you the producers were desperate to get you."

"Well, they have me."

"I thought *I* had you."

This woman was going to end him. They'd just made love for over an hour in the cottage and he already needed her again.

"They have my acting skills. You get everything else."

"Mmm, is that a promise?" What he told her earlier wasn't a lie; he knew he didn't deserve a second chance with this woman, but he did not plan to waste it.

"That's absolutely a promise. What do you think about staying at my place tonight?" he asked as he ran his hands over her pert backside. "I can drive you to the airport tomorrow, before I head back here."

"If you make it worth my while, Mr. Montez." Damn but her hands were like fire on his skin.

"If anyone saw you looking at me with those big gray eyes, they'd have no idea what those hands were getting up to this morning."

She laughed wickedly in response as she stroked him.

"Maybe I'll give you a preview of my plans for the evening now," he suggested, already moving them toward the couch. "I'd love a replay of your lips wrapped around my co—"

"Here you are!" his mother called, then screamed, covering her eyes. "Oh, my God, Gaelito, take your hands off that poor girl. She hasn't even had breakfast yet." That caused Perla to dissolve into fits of laughter, while Gael tried to use her as a shield for his raging erection.

"Mami! Can you give me a minute?"

"Take five, mijo," his mother said reproachingly as she gestured toward Perla. "Ven, Perlita. I want to spend a little more time with you before you leave us. And you better get yourself together, little boy. I don't want to hear about you getting all handsy in that car. That black ice is dangerous out here."

"Fine," he called after his mother, who was already walking out of the room with Perla. He'd come into the house while Perla was packing up and let his mother know he was going into the city with her. To his surprise, she'd been all for it. She told him she was in support of anything that kept him smiling like that. He couldn't disagree. Gael could not wait to finally get Perla alone for a few hours somewhere where there were not nosy relatives underfoot. And once he did, he was going to make sure she understood that he was willing to do whatever it took to make things between them work. And then he'd make it clear to Manolo that his priorities had changed. His sister and mother were right. It was about time he was a little selfish.

Sixteen

Perla looked at Gael's phone, which flashed with yet another incoming call from his uncle. But if he noticed the phone vibrating in the console between their bucket seats, he did not show it. He kept his eyes on the road as he drove her SUV into Manhattan.

"Seems like Manolo really needs to talk to you," she told him as casually as possible. She didn't want to pry, but from what she'd overheard earlier, things sounded tense. Not that he gave any indication that he was having second thoughts about *The Liberator and His Love*. On the contrary, they'd talked about his ideas regarding the role for a decent part of the two-hour drive into the city.

"Do you remember when you did that monologue junior year?" she asked out of nowhere, and instantly saw a change come over his face. The tightness around his mouth that had been there since he'd spoken with Manolo smoothed, and his beautiful lips turned up into a wide smile.

"*You* remember that?" he countered, clearly surprised, and soon she was smiling, too.

"Of course I do. You brought the house down." At the beginning of their junior year all the drama majors were asked to perform a five-minute monologue for the incoming freshmen. Gael picked a scene from *Chronicle of a Death Foretold* by Gabriel García Márquez, and controversially decided to do it in the original Spanish. Perla remembered being in the front row, feeling jittery with nerves for him. Not because she didn't think he'd nail it, but because it felt important. "You were magical that night."

She turned to look at him, remembering the not-quite boy, but not full-grown man he'd been then. How he'd had people on the edge of their seats as he acted out the scene. Magnetic as he moved around the stage, and there hadn't been a single person who wasn't riveted by his presence. She remembered thinking, *He's going to bring our culture to the world. He'll be one of the precious few who get to do that.* And now he really would, and this time she wouldn't just get to see him; she'd be there working with him.

On impulse she reached for her phone, remembering she kept a ton of old videos on an app. After a few taps she had it. She connected her phone to the car's Bluetooth, hit Play and instantly the car was filled with Gael's impassioned voice as he performed García Márquez. His eyes widened almost comically as he realized what he was listening to.

"You still have this?" he asked, struggling to keep his attention on the road. "This isn't fair. I have to focus on the road and can't properly react to the magnificence of twenty-one-year-old me!" She laughed, certain he was only partly teasing, because this man had a lot of wonderful qualities, but humility about his acting skills was not one of them. And even that she'd always loved about him. That he knew the gift he had and tirelessly worked to hone it, to learn how to wield it better.

"You've always been so humble," she joked and leaned in to kiss him as the sound of his voice filled the car. They listened to the clip until it was over, and she was surprised to feel her tear ducts tingling at the crescendo.

"I'm glad you're doing this," she said as she reached for his hand.

"*We're* doing this," he countered, and she heard the scratchiness of emotion in his voice, too, as her own heart bounced in her chest like a rubber ball. For a second, he took his eyes off the road and turned to her. The certainty in his gaze seemed to cauterize any doubt she had about his intentions. They *would* do this, together.

"Are you sure you don't need to get back? Veronica only gets you for a few more days before you have to go on your press tour," Perla asked distractedly as Gael kissed his way down from her collarbone to the swell of her breasts.

After a quick stop at her place so she could repack, they'd come to his apartment. They'd barely gotten in the door before he took her in his arms and started ravaging her.

"My mother is ecstatic that I've escorted my girlfriend up to the city and will be even more ecstatic when I get back tomorrow and let her know when she gets to see you again."

Perla's insides hardly knew what was happening to them anymore. From hour to hour she was awash in emotions. And even if she was certain that Gael's intentions to keep things going between them were sincere, she wasn't so far gone she didn't know they had a challenge ahead of them. She lived in Manhattan and even if he had an apartment here, too, he spent most of his time in LA. Not to mention all the traveling he did for work. Hell, last year he spent most of his time filming in Croatia. To his chagrin she slid out of his arms and got enough distance to have an actual conversation.

"Nope. I keep letting you hypnotize me with your mouth, but we need to talk," she declared as seriously as she could manage, given that he was chasing her around his well-appointed living room with Frankenstein arms and whispering "give us a kiss, love"—in an admittedly pretty decent British accent. "I'm not letting you promise your mother anything on my behalf until we discuss exactly how we're going to do this. We both have busy lives and melding them won't be easy." The last bit sobered Gael up. He leaned against the breakfast counter dividing the kitchen from the rest of the room and raised an eyebrow.

"I want this to work," he told her as if it was all it took.

"It's not just up to us," she said, her arms across her chest, trying to stay strong, because right now with him looking at her like that, he could probably talk her into anything. "Your uncle is not happy about the project, and he's not the type to—"

He didn't even let her finish. "I'll handle Manolo. Don't worry about him. I promise," he said with such confidence, she couldn't not believe him. "Why don't I go down and get some stuff to make you dinner. It is Christmas, after all." He hiked a thumb over his shoulder at the glass cabinet holding floor-to-ceiling rows of wine. "Why don't you pick something for us to drink, and by the time you get comfortable I'll be back with ingredients for asopao de camarones."

"Fine, bribe me with my favorite food," she said, trying and failing to not sound utterly besotted. He brought her into his arms, and she went, even if she knew the conversation he kept deflecting absolutely needed to happen. The real world would not stay at bay for much longer. But it was Christmas and this man wanted to feed her and then make love to her before she had to leave him, and she was going to take this gift she'd been given.

Seventeen

"Are you back already?" Perla looked up from the book she'd been reading and jumped off the couch when she saw Gael's uncle standing just a few yards away. Something about the way he ran his eyes over her made her want to cover herself up, even when she was wearing leggings and a sweater that practically reached her chin.

"Manolo," she said, trying to infuse as much lightness as possible into the name as she stood rooted to the spot by the couch.

"Perla," he said, not even attempting a friendly tone. She'd never liked Manolo. He always seemed to be annoyed by her mere presence, like he wished he could vanish her on sight. Seeing that kind of naked loathing directed at her was disorienting after two days of warmth and affection from Gael's family.

"Feliz Navidad. Gael's out right now," she told the older man, attempting to at least get him to say something.

"I'm not here to see my nephew." He smiled coldly. "I wanted a word with you," he told her as he moved farther inside the apartment. Gael had purchased his two-bedroom in the iconic Calabria building a few years earlier and even though it was tastefully renovated, it was not very big. "I assumed you'd be here." The menace in his voice made a shiver run up her spine. "I know my nephew well enough to predict how these things go with him and his lady friends."

Perla felt a wave of nausea at the way he said *lady friends*, but she was not letting Manolo get to her. She and Gael had been together long enough for her to get to know his uncle. He'd always been callous when he was unhappy.

With only a few steps he was practically in front of her and it seemed to Perla that he was taking up all the space in the room. She moved so that the large sectional leather couch acted as a barrier between them. She wasn't going to give him the satisfaction of seeing her cower, though, so she crossed her arms and tipped her chin up.

"How can I help you? If you want to discuss the details of the contract, you'll need to talk to our attorneys. I only get the talent to sign on—what they actually *sign* is out of my jurisdiction," she said, trying for a joke, but landing with a thud.

"He won't care what he gets," Manolo scoffed and the way he furrowed his brows, with an almost piratical slant, reminded her of Gael. Manolo was his father's younger brother, after all. He had the same bronzed skin as her lover, and that imposing size. "Gael is taking this role to get you back. That boy could never think straight whenever you were involved. Did you know he almost threw away his career for you?"

"What?" she asked, her heart accelerating with every word that came out of Manolo's mouth.

"He kept turning jobs down because he was constantly having to deal with you and your drama. He almost declined that show with Shapiro after you called him crying about your mother bullying you at some party on a yacht or some other nonsense." The series directed by Arnold Shapiro had been Gael's breakout role. It premiered only six months after their college graduation. And that night on the yacht had been one of the most humiliating of her life. Someone asked her about Gael in front of her mother and Carmelina had laughed out loud and said, "He's probably with his real girlfriend."

Manolo's cruel laugh snatched Perla out of the awful memory, but the twisted anger in his face didn't make her feel much better. "I had to beg him to take the part, and when he realized the chance he'd almost blown because of you, he finally saw that you would end his career before he'd even started."

"I never asked him—"

He kept yelling, like she hadn't even opened her

mouth. "You don't understand the sacrifices we all made for Gael to get where he is. The multiple jobs his mother and I had to take to help him and Gabi with tuition."

"I know that—"

"What could you possibly know about struggling to make ends meet?" he sneered, making shame roil inside her. "You were born with a silver spoon in your mouth, and then you caught your showpiece. That was all he was going to be to your family if he'd stayed with you. A pretty boy you brought to parties." Manolo glowered as Perla tried to muster up something to say. "You don't think I know what your mother said about him? You don't think she called me up to demand I keep Gael in check because he didn't have the pedigree to date a Sambrano?"

"She did what?" Perla asked, amazed that her mother's disgusting behavior still managed to surprise her.

Manolo let out another one of those chilly laughs. "Oh, yeah, and to think he almost threw everything away for you, just so your mother could look at him like he was trash when you brought him home. Our family is not like yours, Perla. There is no trust fund to fall back on. Gael has people depending on him."

"I didn't know my mother had done that. I'm sorry," she said numbly, head spinning.

"Oh, your mother did more than that." The smile on his face was pure ice. "Your mother had one of her lawyers call me up and offer me money to get Gael away from you."

"What?" she heard herself say, and she had to lean on the back of the couch just to keep from sinking to the ground.

"It was a nice chunk of change, too," he said casually. "But I'm not for sale and neither is Gael. In this family we work for what we have, and if we have to make hard decisions in the process, then that is what we do. When you were trying to play house with Gael he was building a career to help himself and his family, and you put that in jeopardy." That was a jab, but she could scarcely feel it. The shame and humiliation from what her mother had done made her feel like she'd been coated in slime.

"You've been back on the scene for days and he's already being reckless. His mother's medical bills cost him hundreds of thousands of dollars already and there will mostly likely be more. That mansion he bought her needs to be paid off by working. He can't afford to turn down roles so he can chase after you. He's taking this role and turning down a good opportunity because he feels guilty, not because it's what his career needs. He's giving up millions for you. That has consequences. My reputation and Gael's will take a hit for this."

"But he said he hadn't committed to anything," Perla said in a daze. But Manolo was right; she knew how things were in Hollywood. It didn't take much for an actor to get a reputation for "being flaky" and soon offers started drying up. Latinx actors could not afford to be seen as unreliable. Manolo was an ass, but he wasn't wrong.

"You've always been that boy's weakness. He almost sank himself once before to keep you and he'll do it again. Are you willing to live with that, Perla?"

This hurt, so much she couldn't get air in her lungs, but she could not deny the truth in what he was saying. Hell, an hour ago she'd been wondering how she and Gael could even make their relationship work. She should've stuck to the plan. She should've let everything end when she left the Hamptons, but once again her desire for Gael had made her lie to herself, and this time at least she could walk away with some dignity. She knew he'd be hurt, but this was for the best. Eventually, he'd understand.

"Okay," she told Manolo. She moved like a sleepwalker to the spot next to the doorway where her small suitcase was still sitting. She grabbed her coat and her purse and moved to the door. "I think I'm going to go back to my place. I'll call my sister and tell her we'll have to go with another actor."

"This is for the best, Perla," Manolo called after her as she shut the door behind her. She had no one to blame for this but herself. And now she'd have to clean up the mess she'd made.

"Did you open a bottle already? Because I found the Albariño you liked at dinner last night." Gael walked into his apartment and almost dropped the two bags of food he was carrying when he found his uncle on his couch with a glass of Scotch in his hand.

"Where's Perla, Tío?" he asked as he put down

the bags and went to the hallway leading to the bedrooms. "Babe?"

"She's gone, mijo."

Gael whipped his head back to look at his uncle, sure he'd misheard. Gone? Where would she go? He'd left her reading a book not even an hour ago.

"Gone where?" he asked suspiciously. Something was very wrong, and he suspected it had everything to do with the fact that Manolo was sitting in his apartment in Manhattan and not at the house in Sagaponack.

"What is going on, Manolo?" he asked, not even attempting to tamp down the anger that was already bubbling up. "I thought you were going to the Hamptons."

"I had to come and fix this." He said it like barging into Gael's uninvited was a big fucking imposition. "I knew you wouldn't do it, not again."

"Fix what? What the hell are you talking about, Manolo?"

His uncle let out a long-suffering sigh, because apparently explaining how he'd run off Perla from the apartment was a big chore.

"I told her the truth. That *The Liberator and His Love* is not a good move for your career. That your mother's illness has and will continue to cost a fortune and you have your whole family depending on you." He gave him that wise fatherly look that always made Gael's blood boil. "We've been here before. I know you care for the girl, but they're not like us. Remember what her mother tried to do."

There it was, the reminder that Carmelina Sambrano had tried to blackmail Manolo to keep Gael away from Perla, and he'd turned it down. One of the many things his uncle used as currency to remind Gael what a saint he was. He'd always thought his uncle pushed him out of love, out of wanting what was best for him, but now he saw that this was all manipulation. "Gael, deep down you know I'm right, son."

"Don't call me son!" he yelled, stepping up to his uncle so that he was only inches away from his face. He didn't even try to check his fury. If Manolo was man enough to come into his house and do this, then he could deal with the consequences. "The only person in this world that has a right to call me that is Veronica Montez."

Manolo's eyes widened as if finally realizing that he had not played his cards right.

For a moment Gael thought of a time-lapse video he'd seen of a lake icing over. That was how his anger felt now, like it was filling him from head to toe.

"How did I not see what you've been doing?" Gael asked, shaking with rage. "This has never been about me and my happiness. It's about you keeping the golden calf as fat as possible."

"How could you say that? After all I've done—"

"Enough!" Gael roared, cutting Manolo's falsehoods off. He was so close to doing something he'd regret. He was fighting to get himself under control when his phone rang. He almost let it go to voice mail, but decided against it in case it was Perla.

When he fished it out of his pocket he saw it was his sister and answered anyway, hoping Gabi would distract him from punching his uncle in the face.

"Is Perla with you?"

"No. She's gone, thanks to Manolo," he growled as his uncle stood up. His sister sounded frantic, her voice so loud Manolo heard her, and when the man made a move to come closer, Gael held up a hand. If his uncle got too close he wouldn't be responsible for what he did. He'd been raised to respect his elders, but his mother had also taught him that people needed to earn that respect. In the last few minutes, he'd lost every ounce he'd ever had for Manolo.

"Dammit, Gael, are you listening to me?" Gabi's loud voice brought Gael back to the moment, and what she said sank in. "Can you say that again?" he asked, feeling like his mind might shatter from the blind rage he was feeling.

"Bro, I did a little digging around and it looks like this project Tio has been trying to talk you into is with Baxter Jones."

Baxter Jones, the Hollywood mogul currently under investigation for dozens of allegations of sexual assault. Gael would rather lose his career than work with that man. "What are you talking about? I saw the name of the production company. It's not him."

His sister exhaled and when she spoke, her voice was wooden. "That's the thing. Apparently, he's set up this one as a front so people don't connect it to him, but it's his money. And, G, my friend said

Manolo took a kickback from them in exchange for a guarantee that you would join the project. That's why he's been so pressed about you taking the Sambrano project instead. He took a bribe from them."

"I'll call you back."

"Wait! We're on our way to you."

"You're what! Gabriela, for fuck's sake."

"Mami had a bad feeling when Tio said he couldn't come out today, and you know how she gets. She wouldn't stop fussing until I agreed to drive her over to make sure everything was okay. We'll stay at my place."

"Fine. I have to go. I need to take care of this." Fury boiled over in Gael until he shook with it. He slammed the phone on the breakfast counter so hard he was sure he'd shattered the screen.

"You," he garbled out as he stalked toward his uncle, "associated my name with a sexual predator. You chased away the woman I love for money?" Gael looked at his uncle, and it was like he was seeing him for the first time. He was older now in his fifties, but he still was a big man, imposing. Manolo was used to getting his way, of cajoling and pushing boundaries until he obtained the results he wanted. And over the years Gael had let his uncle sway him just to keep the peace, but this time he had gone too far. "This was never about my career, was it?" he demanded as he fought for control. "You just wanted money. It's not enough that you've made millions off me, but now you're taking kickbacks and whoring me out to work for a literal monster. Do you know

what working with Baxter would do to my career,
Manolo?" Gael knew he was screaming; he probably looked terrifying, but control was beyond him.
The betrayal and the panic of having lost Perla again
was driving a rage in him that he'd never felt before.

"I did it for you," Manolo pleaded, his eyes wide
with fear. But Gael knew he wasn't what scared his
uncle. What scared Manolo was knowing he was
about to lose access to his money. Still, he tried.

"You were never going to stay with that girl. You
know how we are. The Montez men are no good to
women. Per—"

"Don't," Gael barked, blood roaring in his ears.
"Don't you dare even say her name," he said as he
jabbed a finger in the direction of his uncle. "And
do not pretend for a second this has anything to do
with me or Perla. You did this all for yourself, just
like my father used his tired excuses to justify his
own selfishness. You have been dangling the help
you gave my mother over my head for too long, and
you know what?" Gael bared his teeth as he got so
close to his uncle he could see the man's jaw trembling. "I think I've more than paid back what we
owed you. I'm going to go look for Perla now, and
when I come back you better not be here."

Manolo stumbled as he tried and failed to act
like everything was fine. "Sure, I'll just let you sort
things out and we can talk in a couple of days."

Gael was already grabbing his keys from the hallway table when he answered his uncle. "No, you

don't understand, Manolo. I can't have someone who I don't trust managing my career. You're fired."

With that, Gael stepped out of his apartment and got in the elevator, sick with the fear that he may have lost her for good this time. He'd suspected it from the first moment he saw her getting out of that SUV, he'd been almost sure when he'd danced with her in his mother's living room, but now he was certain. He'd never stopped loving Perla; his heart had been frozen these past six years. Life, success, fame washing over him while he walked around numb. Because he didn't have the one person in his life who made him stop and look around. The person who made him want to live for himself. And just when he'd gotten her back, she had slipped from his fingers again.

Eighteen

"Come in," Perla called when she heard a soft knock on her bedroom door. Well, bedroom didn't exactly do the space justice; it was more like a luxury suite. Her sister and her fiancé had purchased this villa in Punta Cana a year ago and it was magnificent. It was a ten-thousand-square-foot home done in a minimalist design. Glass and metal covered the facade of the house, so that you could take in the majestic Caribbean Sea from wherever you were standing. Perla's room was done in white and corals, and everything seemed to blend in with the views.

"You're up," her sister, Esmeralda, said as she stepped into the room. It was barely 7 a.m. but Perla hadn't been able to get a lot of sleep.

"Only just." Perla smiled instinctively as she saw

her sister. "I was admiring the view. I can't believe the curtains are able to block all this sunlight," Perla said as she looked at the swaying palm trees beyond her balcony.

"There are pocket doors in the wall that slide out when you hit the button for the blackout curtains. It cost a fortune," she laughed as she came over to the bed and put her arm around Perla's shoulder. "But you know Rodrigo. He wanted the best. And the best was a house where you could see the ocean from every room." Her sister turned to look at Perla, her eyes brimming with a kindness that almost broke her. "How are you *really* doing?"

"I'm not fully sure yet," Perla sighed and closed her eyes as she tried to gather her thoughts. The past eighteen hours had been terrible, but she at least had landed in a place where everyone welcomed her with open arms. She'd left Gael's apartment and gone to the parking garage where they'd left her car and sat in it for what felt like hours. And then she started driving. She'd ended up at JFK. She'd bought a first-class ticket on the next flight to Punta Cana and sat in the airport for four hours, waiting. Gael had attempted to call her, leaving her multiple messages begging her to talk to him. He'd told her in those messages that he was sorry for what Manolo had said. That it was not how he felt. He pleaded with her to let him come to her.

But she hadn't responded to a single one. Eventually, after she got ahold of Esmeralda and told her she'd arrive late in the evening instead of the next morning, she powered off her phone. She'd kept it off until she opened her eyes a few minutes before Esmeralda had knocked on her door, but there had been no more calls from Gael. Maybe he realized his uncle was right and decided she was still a liability, after all.

"I'm not sure if Gael will be doing the Rios project anymore," she confessed. "I'm sorry, Esmeralda. It's all my fault."

Perla braced herself for her sister's reaction. Esmeralda had never been anything but supportive of her, but this was a major fumble. And it was all because Perla had not been able to keep her feelings out of the situation. She'd lied to herself about faking the relationship with Gael. She hadn't been pretending for a second. From the moment she'd seen him he'd gotten right under her skin. Like he always did. And now she'd messed up in her first big project for the studio.

"First of all, nothing is your fault," Esmeralda assured Perla. Her sister's eyes were so kind. There wasn't a semblance of anger or even slight frustration as she spoke. "Second, there's no problem. Jimena in legal texted this morning to say that Gael's new manager emailed last night saying they were reviewing and would send the contract back promptly."

"His *new* manager?" Perla asked, surprised.

"Yes," Esme said brightly as she gave Perla another squeeze. "Looks like his sister, Gabriela, is in that role now. As far as Jimena was concerned, Mr. Montez seems very committed to everything related to this project and whatever he promised you." Perla's head snapped up to look at her sister. Something in the way Esmeralda said the last part made her heart kick up in her chest.

"Did they say why they were still interested? As far as I know this was not financially as good an offer as the other he was considering," Perla said in a subdued tone.

"I didn't get a lot of details, but Gael is no dummy, and from what Jimena told me, neither is his sister. But they have not even hinted at pulling out."

Perla's head felt like it was spinning. She was certain that Gael would come back to his place, find her gone and decide it was all for the best. That he'd side with Manolo and go with the project that would make him more money. But he...hadn't.

"I didn't think he'd take it," she told Esmeralda, her gaze on the cerulean waters in the distance.

"Can I ask you something?"

Perla rolled her eyes at her sister's question, then nodded.

"Would you take a second chance on him?"

There was no point in even asking who the *him* was. There had only ever been one *him* where she was concerned. And she wished that the answer to that question took her longer to figure out. That was a door she should never again want to see open. The agony of losing him the first time should have made her hesitate, and yet the only word on her tongue was *yes*.

"Gael is too much of a professional to back out

of a commitment, but that doesn't mean he has any intention of carrying on with me." And even saying that felt like a betrayal, because he'd told her he did. She'd had to leave, there was no way she could stay in that apartment with Manolo, after the things he'd said, but she couldn't deny that she wondered if she should've picked up the phone when Gael called, heard him out.

Her sister looked at her and shook her head sadly. "You know what was the biggest lesson I learned last year when Rodrigo and I were at each other's throats for the CEO position?"

"That my mother and brother are horrible people?" Esme clicked her tongue at that and reached for her hand.

"I learned that when life gives you a path forward you have two choices: get on it with all your old baggage dragging you down, or you can leave that stuff behind and walk into your fresh start with a lighter load. And you know what's the best part of shedding some of that deadweight?"

"What?" Perla asked, even if she suspected she knew the answer.

"That you'll have room for a companion." Before she could even fully let Esme's words sink in, a clear image of her walking hand in hand with Gael appeared in her mind like a memory.

"You know what?" Esme asked, breaking Perla out of her thoughts. "I think we should do a sleepover on the yacht. Just the two of us."

"You do?" Perla wasn't exactly surprised; the

yacht had been a wedding present Rodrigo and Esme had gotten each other. They would spend their honeymoon on it a few months from now. Even if Perla wasn't in the mood, Esmeralda's excitement was infectious, and she could use a day or two focusing on something other than her mixed-up emotions.

"Let's do it," she said with as much enthusiasm as she could manage, which admittedly was not a whole lot.

"Excellent." Esme clapped in excitement. "We'll head over there before dinner. My mom has plans for a beach day and would kill me if I steal you from her and the tias."

Perla didn't believe for a second that Esme was put out about spending time with her mother and aunts. Esmeralda adored those women and she took every chance she got to pamper them. "We'll give them the morning and afternoon. We can party like rock stars in the evening," she told her with a wink. "I'll have the chef make us some treats."

As she watched her older sister walk away already talking into her phone, Perla wished she could muster up more enthusiasm, but all she wanted was to curl up in her bed and cry. Losing Gael a second time hurt as much as she'd known it would.

"So what's your plan again?" Gabi was leaning against the door frame, watching him frantically pack a bag.

"I am going to grovel and let her know I made the biggest mistake of my life when I let Manolo convince me she was a liability all those years ago. And then I'll do whatever it takes to convince her that I would give up everything for her, including my career."

"Okay, I like the basics of that plan, but how do you know she wants you there?" his twin sister asked as she pulled her phone out of her pocket. "Do you even have a flight secured?"

"Yes, Gabriela," Gael snapped as he zipped his small bag. "I called the crew and they have the jet ready at the Westchester airport. We fly out in a couple of hours. And I've been in touch with Esmeralda."

"Sambrano?" Gabi inquired, obviously surprised.

"Yes, you're not the only one who can call people. I reached out to her when I couldn't find Perla. We've been talking and she told me that she wouldn't tell me where they were until she was sure Perla wanted to see me. But she texted and said she thought Perla would be up for talking to me. So I'm flying down there."

"And what are you telling her once you get there, son?" His mother challenged him as she shuffled into his bedroom, because his sister, his mother and his grandmother were all in his house. Not one of them, as they promised they would, had left him alone. They'd stayed with him all day and watched him pace his apartment when he couldn't find Perla. They'd all reminded him a thousand times that he deserved to be happy. That Perla loved him, too. That all wasn't lost. It had been good to have them there.

Gael turned to his mother. She still looked frail wrapped in his robe, but he knew the steel that hid in those brown eyes. Manolo had helped with money, that was true, but his mother had raised him in every way that counted.

"I'm going to tell her I love her, Mami," he stated and felt the truth of those words settle in him. "I just hope I deserve her."

His mother walked up to him and placed her hands on either side of his face. "I want you to hear me. Your father was who he was, and no matter what you think that means, I want you to remember that you're half mine. I raised you and you're a good man. The best." She poked his chest, and he let out a yelp, making her laugh. "Believe that, mijo."

He wondered how his mother had known that it was exactly what he needed to hear. For so long he'd believed there was something in him that would eventually break Perla's heart. And there had been. But it wasn't a curse. It was his own insecurity. It was him letting his past dictate his present. He was done with that.

"I believe it, Ma," he assured her.

"Good," his mother told him as she kissed him on the cheek. "Now, go get your girl, mijo. We'll be here waiting for you both when you get back."

Nineteen

"Here we are. We have a slip on the end. We needed the extra space because we fancy," Esme said with a waggle of her eyebrows as she maneuvered the car in the parking lot of the marina. "I'm excited about this and you look great," her sister said, gesturing at Perla's black maxi dress and her silver sandals. She had to admit it was very nice to switch from snowy New York to beach weather.

"I'm looking forward to taking my mind off..." She didn't even know where to start. It would be impossible to not think about Gael. He was ever present in her mind. It was like she thought about him even when she didn't. Everything she saw, heard, smelled somehow reminded her of him. Or reminded her that she missed him, that she'd almost had him and she'd lost him again. Since those initial attempts to reach her, he hadn't called, not even once. She wished it didn't hurt like it did. She'd tried so hard to convince herself she was past this. And she knew she wasn't the same insecure, lonely girl who had fallen for Gael.

She was different now, stronger. She knew that. She *felt* that. It just so happened that this new version of her loved him, too. She couldn't deny that fact any more than she could deny her own name. That man had always felt like he'd been made for her. Even when she felt inconsequential and undesirable, he looked at her like she was all he could see. And one didn't forget being wanted like that.

"Perlita, did you hear me?" Her sister's voice jolted her out of her thoughts, and she realized she'd been sitting there staring out the windshield.

"Sorry," she said, more than a little embarrassed. "My mind keeps drifting."

"Pobrecita," Esmeralda clucked like a mother hen, and leaned to pat her cheek. "It'll be okay. I promise." Perla tried her best to smile at her sister's optimism, but knew she likely looked more like she was in pain. "Here, why don't you head over to the boat. I just need to make a call. I'll be right behind you," Esme said as she tapped something on her phone.

Perla laughed at her sister calling a fifteen-million-dollar yacht a *boat*.

"Your boat has a gym, five staterooms and a swimming pool, but okay, sis."

Esme grinned at that. "*Our* boat, Perlita. Rodrigo and I want our family to enjoy it, and you're family."

Perla felt a stone lodge in her throat as tears filled her eyes. It was such a small thing to say, probably just out of politeness, but it meant so much. She'd needed to hear it. It's not like she'd never been on a yacht. Her father's was in a berth in a marina in Florida. But she was no longer welcome to use that. Her mother had been more than clear. Not that she'd miss it; there were too many bad memories attached to it. Like so many things connected to her mother.

"Go, the crew is expecting you. It's right at the end of the dock." Perla noticed that Esme was looking a little frazzled as she read the message that had just come in on her phone and wondered if something was wrong.

"Are you sure? I can wait for you."

Her sister beamed at her as she nodded. "I'm sure. Rodrigo just wanted to get some details about the honeymoon. You know how he is." Esme winked, and Perla laughed. Rodrigo was devoted to Esmeralda. The man worshipped the ground her sister walked on. She couldn't even be jealous of what they had. It was too pure. That didn't mean that she didn't feel a pang of yearning in her chest at the reminder that she'd never have that. Gael's career would always come first.

"Okay, I'll see you there," she told her sister after she opened the car door. She grabbed her purse and her hat as her sister gestured in the direction she should go.

"That way, and don't worry about the bags. One of the crew will get them and bring them aboard."

Perla took a moment to take in the ocean breeze and the beauty of the place. She'd always had a loose and complicated connection to her father's homeland. But now it felt like she was turning a new page here, too. As she made her way up the dock, she spotted the yacht. It wasn't exactly easy to miss. It was sleek and imposing, the biggest vessel on the dock. Perla noticed a man on the bridge headed toward the walkway. He looked...no. Perla stopped in her tracks, sure that her eyes were playing tricks on her. It couldn't be. She was still about fifty yards away and the sun was setting. It was probably the crew member coming to get their bags.

But the moment she saw him step on the walkway, she knew it was him.

"What?" she exclaimed as she turned around. Her sister, that traitor, was standing by the door of her Cayenne, grinning from ear to ear. "Did you do this?" Perla yelled, too spooked to turn back around and face him. Her heart had given up on pounding and was now doing triple somersaults in her chest. She felt like she wanted to run, then scream, then pass out.

Esme just shook her head and pointed at something over Perla's shoulder. "He did it! I just helped. Go get your man, Perlita!"

She felt him before he said a word. His presence big and undeniable at her back. It has always been like that with him. She could sense Gael in a room before she ever laid eyes on him. Like her entire being was attuned to his presence.

"Can you turn around, baby?" She could feel the warmth of him all the way down her body, and after taking one long and deep breath she moved to face him.

"You're here," she breathed out, taking him in, larger than life, almost too beautiful to be real. Her fallen angel. The man who had never stopped owning her heart.

She could see the emotions displayed all over his face. The way his eyes scanned over her. As if reassuring himself that she was really there. The way he gnawed on his bottom lip made her want to reach for him.

"I'm so sorry, mi amor," he told her as their eyes locked. "I wish I could go back and erase everything that I've ever done or allowed someone else to do to hurt you."

"You don't need—"

"No, please," he pleaded, taking her in his arms. "Please let me say this. I *need* to say this. There hasn't been a moment in the last six years that I didn't feel that something essential was gone from me. I didn't have the tools to deserve you back then, and I probably don't have all that I need now, but I swear to you. Perla, if you let me, I will spend the rest of my life striving to be the man you need."

Without a word she jumped so that her legs were wrapped around his waist. She pressed her forehead to his and breathed in the scent of him. That thing that was uniquely him and that she *always* craved. "I never wanted perfection, Gael. All I ever wanted was you." His breath hitched at her words and in the background she was pretty sure she heard her older sister whooping in delight.

"We're making a scene," she muttered as she hid her face in his neck.

"What good is being a movie star if I can't give the woman I love a fairy-tale ending?" Gael asked in a teasing voice.

"I don't need a fairy tale, Gael," she told him as she looked into his eyes.

"What if I want to give it to you anyway?" he asked as he turned to walk them up to the awaiting yacht, and Perla thought she might actually have a chance to get everything she ever wanted, and she was finally ready to let herself believe she deserved all of it.

Epilogue

"Are you ready for this, mi vida?" Gael asked as he looked out the window of their Escalade while they waited their turn in the long line of cars dropping off a good portion of Hollywood's A-list at the evening's red-carpet event.

"I am absolutely ready," she assured him, brushing a kiss on his cheek before leaning in to look at the crowd outside. Right beyond the car she could see the throng of paparazzi and journalists waiting as couples dressed in their awards-season finery stepped out of limousines and SUVs, posing for the cameras. Tonight Gael was up for a best actor nomination for his performance of Francisco Rios, and the series *The Liberator and His Love* had garnered over ten nominations. Their small project about the life and love of the Puerto Rican liberator had turned out to be an enormous financial and critical success. And now she got to walk out into the spotlight hand in hand with the man of her dreams—with her future husband.

Perla smiled as she lifted her left hand where a beautiful vintage Van Cleef & Arpels engagement ring sat on her finger. Gael had proposed over Thanksgiving at his Hamptons home surrounded by his family and her sister. Perla grinned, remembering how she'd gasped when he'd shown her the ring. A platinum band with a perfect black pearl at the center surrounded by a halo of ten old-cut diamonds. It was delicate and elegant, and perfect for her. Just like he was. Just like their life together was.

"We're here, Mr. Montez, Miss Sambrano." The low voice of their driver brought her attention back to the moment. Gael tugged on her right hand and winked as he looked down at her other hand, which was still suspended in the air.

"It's showtime, baby."

Perla took a deep breath and grabbed the clutch bag that matched her gown. Late January in LA meant sunny weather with a bite, but she would have to brave the few minutes on the red carpet with her shoulders completely bare. Anything for fashion. She'd gone with a vintage Charles James clover gown in gold, and on her ears and neck she had a few hundred thousand dollars' worth of sapphires, courtesy of Bulgari. To Perla's absolute delight, her jewelry matched Gael's custom Tom Ford tux. He looked devastatingly handsome, as always.

He'd gotten a haircut to play his part as Rios and decided he would keep the style. His brown hair was cut close to the scalp on the side and back and longer on the top. It suited him, although who was she kidding? The man looked good in everything, and she was not going to pinch herself again. This really was her life, and she deserved all of it. Including the absolutely perfect man with whom she was about to walk the red carpet.

"Let's do this," she declared, already moving. As Gael helped her down from the car, she smiled at the cameras frantically flashing in her face.

What a difference two years made.

Well, two years and a month if you wanted to get specific. After Gael had come to the DR and they'd decided to give each other another chance, time had gone by in a flash. They both had their demanding jobs, and blending all that took time. But they'd managed to prioritize the life they were building together and Perla had never been happier. They were both bicoastal now and making it work, and they'd even been seeing a couple's therapist for the past year, which had helped them understand each other better. Perla could talk about how her family dynamics had impacted her, and Gael was able to open up regarding the wounds his father's abandonment had left in him. It was wild to think that by now they'd been together as long as they had their first time around. And no, it wasn't always easy, but this time they were building a solid foundation, and she knew that they could weather any storm.

"Can we see the ring, Miss Sambrano?" called the throng of photographers as Gael guided her up the long red carpet. She'd been to awards shows before, but never one of this caliber, and *never* like this. Not with one of the biggest stars in Hollywood by her side and her heart full to the brim with happiness. And definitely not when a show she was a producer on was predicted to sweep the awards season.

Perla lifted her hand in front of her chest and immediately a flurry of camera flashes started bursting in her direction. Gael wrapped his arm around her waist and pressed a kiss to her ear. "You're a trouper, baby."

"It's no hardship to brag that the sexiest man alive according to six different magazines just put a ring on it," she said, inciting a bark of laughter from her fiancé. They kept walking until they were stopped by one of the show hosts who were standing around intercepting celebrities to ask them about their clothes.

"Gael Montez!" beckoned a Latina in a teal mermaid gown Perla recognized from a competing network. There were people walking in all directions and if you even blinked, you ran the chance of missing a Hollywood living legend passing by.

"Hey, Sandra," Gael said, leaning in for a kiss, then gestured to Perla with a smile. "My fiancée."

"Of course, Miss Sambrano, congratulations on the engagement," she cried as she tried to commandeer a corner for all three of them to stand. "I'd heard you'd be wearing vintage Charles James today," Sandra exclaimed and made a bowing motion in front of Perla's gown. "Exquisite," the woman exclaimed, as she looked at the camera. "All the folks at home, behold the Latinx Power Couple of the moment, Perla Sambrano and Gael Montez." Sandra actually clapped as if they were worthy of a standing ovation.

Perla's stomach fluttered slightly, her nerves getting to her a bit as she took in the moment. And as if he could sense her discomfort, Gael brought Perla closer, pressing her to his side. "How are you feeling for tonight, Gael?" Sandra asked, then turned to Perla. "It could be a big one for you both."

Gael's smile was almost beatific as he looked down at Perla, taking his time before answering the reporter's question. Someday her heart would stop pounding in her chest whenever he looked at her like that, but today there was no helping it. He bent down to brush a kiss to her cheek before he turned his attention on the expectant woman who was looking at them with obvious delight.

"I'm honored for the nomination and immensely proud to be a part of this production. I became an actor with the hope that I could someday get to play a role like this one. To Boricuas, Francisco Rios is more than a legend. He represents the bravery and dignity of our island, and I will always be grateful to the love of my life for convincing me to take the role of a lifetime. But I have to say, I'm already walking in feeling like a winner knowing I get to spend my future with this woman." Perla struggled between almost swooning at Gael's words and blinking furiously in an effort to hold back tears.

"Gael!" she wailed. "You promised you wouldn't make me cry!" That got a laugh from Sandra and the few others who had gathered to watch Gael Montez be interviewed.

"It's true," he told her as he softly kissed her forehead.

"There you have it, folks," Sandra said with a bow as they got ready to move on. "True love at the awards tonight. We wish Mr. Montez and Miss Sambrano the best of luck tonight and for the wedding."

Within moments they were walking the last yards of the red carpet and heading into the foyer of the theater. As soon as they were past security, Gael pulled her into a little alcove where she could catch her breath.

"Are you all right?" he asked as he ran his hands in soothing circles over her back.

She nodded with her head pressed to his chest. "I'm good, even though you made me cry."

She heard the rumble of his laugh, but stayed right where she was, safe and warm in Gael's arms. The only place in the world where she felt completely at ease. "I was only telling the truth. The nomination is an honor, but no matter what I will go home with the greatest treasure I could ever ask for."

"I'm already marrying you," she said, feigning an annoyance that was a sharp contrast to the swarm of butterflies in her stomach.

"Look at me, baby." His fingers gently nudging

her chin until their eyes were locked on each other. "Thank you."

"For what?" she asked breathlessly.

He smiled, shaking his head like she had asked the silliest of questions, and bent down to kiss her. It was a small brushing of lips, but she felt the depth and strength of his love even in that minimal contact. "Thank you for giving me the chance to make you happy."

"I love you," she whispered, certain in their love and the life of happiness that awaited before them.

* * * * *

**WE HOPE YOU ENJOYED
THIS BOOK FROM**

✦HARLEQUIN
DESIRE

*Luxury, scandal, desire—welcome to
the lives of the American elite.*

Be transported to the worlds of oil barons, family dynasties,
moguls and celebrities. Get ready for juicy plot twists,
delicious sensuality and intriguing scandal.

6 NEW BOOKS AVAILABLE EVERY MONTH!

HDHALO2021

#2839 WHAT HE WANTS FOR CHRISTMAS
Westmoreland Legacy: The Outlaws • by Brenda Jackson
After a decade apart, COO Sloan Outlaw isn't looking to get back with ex Lesley Cassidy. But with her company facing a hostile takeover, he offers his assistance...if she joins him at his luxury cabin. But when they find themselves snowed in, the heat ignites...

#2840 HOW TO HANDLE A HEARTBREAKER
Texas Cattleman's Club: Fathers and Sons • by Joss Wood
Gaining independence from her wealthy family, officer and law student Hayley Lopez is rarely intimidated, especially by the likes of billionaire playboy developer Jackson Michaels. An advocate for the underdog, Hayley clashes often with Jackson. But will one hot night together change everything?

#2841 THE WRONG MR. RIGHT
Dynasties: The Carey Center • by Maureen Child
For contractor Hannah Yates, the offer to work on CEO Bennett Carey's project is a boon. Hired to repair his luxury namesake restaurant, she finds his constant presence and good looks...distracting. Burned before, she won't lose focus, but the sparks between them can't be ignored...

#2842 HOLIDAY PLAYBOOK
Locketts of Tuxedo Park • by Yahrah St. John
Advertising exec Giana Lockett has a lot to prove to her football dynasty family, and landing sports drink CEO Wynn Starks's account is crucial. But their undeniable attraction is an unforeseen complication. Will they be able to make the winning play to save their relationship and business deal?

#2843 INCONVENIENT ATTRACTION
The Eddington Heirs • by Zuri Day
When wealthy businessman Cayden Barker is blindsided by Avery Gray, it's not just by her beauty—her car accidently hits his. And then they meet again unexpectedly—at the country club where he's a member and she's employed. Is this off-limits match meant to last?

#2844 BACKSTAGE BENEFITS
Devereaux Inc. • by LaQuette
TV producer Josiah Manning needs to secure lifestyle guru Lyric Smith as host of his new show. As tempting as the offer—and producer—is, Lyric is hesitant. But as a rival emerges, will they take the stage together or let the curtain fall on their sizzling chemistry?

"What do you want to ask me, Sloan?"

He drew in a deep breath. "I need to know what made you come looking for me last night."

She broke eye contact with him and glanced out the window, not saying anything for a moment. "You were gone longer than you said you would be. I got worried. It was either go see what was taking you so long or pace the floor with worry even more. I chose the former."

"But the weather had turned into a blizzard, Les." He then realized he'd called her what he'd normally called her while they'd been together. She had been Les and not Leslie.

"I know that. I also knew you were out there in it. I tried to convince myself that you could take care of yourself, but I also knew with the amount of wind blowing and snow coming down that anything could have happened."

She paused again before saying, "Chances are, you would have made it back to the cabin, but I couldn't risk the chance you would not have."

He tried not to concentrate on the sadness he heard in her voice and saw in her eyes. Instead, he concentrated on her mouth and in doing so was reminded of just how it tasted. "Not sure if I would have made it back, Les. My head was hurting, and it was getting harder and harder to make my body move because I was so cold. Hell, I wasn't even sure I was going in the right direction. I regret you put your own life at risk, but I'm damn glad you were there when I needed you."

"Just like you were there for me and my company when I needed you, Sloan," she said softly.

Her words made him realize that they'd been there for each other when it had mattered the most. He didn't want to think what would have been the outcome if he'd been at the cabin alone as originally planned and the snowstorm hit. Nor did he want to think what would have happened to her and her company if Redford hadn't told him what was going on. The potential outcome of either made him shiver.

"You're still cold. I'd better go and get that hot chocolate going," she said, shifting to get up and reach for her clothes.

"Don't go yet," he said, not ready for any distance to be put between them or their bodies.

She glanced over at him. Their gazes held and then, as if she'd just noticed his erection pressing against her thigh, she said, "You do know the only reason why we're naked in this sleeping bag together, right?"

He nodded. "Yes. Because I needed your body's heat last night." He inched his mouth closer to hers and then said, "Only problem is, I still need your body's heat, Les. But now I need it for a totally different reason."

And then he leaned in and kissed her.

Don't miss what happens next in...
What He Wants for Christmas *by Brenda Jackson,*
the next book in her Westmoreland Legacy:
The Outlaws series!

Available December 2021 wherever
Harlequin Desire books and ebooks are sold.

Harlequin.com

HDEXP1121